"Now you know all about me," Mac said

"Does it make you any happier?"

Olivia regarded him with dismay. The man she had married had gone. The coldhearted stranger had returned. "No," she answered at last. "You can't deny you married me on the rebound."

His lips twisted. "After eighteen months, hardly a rebound."

"Well then, why did you marry me?"

His eyes wandered over her, his hands reached to caress her. "Propinquity. You were there, an attractive young woman. I wanted you. I knew that the only way I could get you was to marry you."

She pushed herself away from him, sobbing. "I hate you, Mac Connal. I wish I'd never come here. I wish I'd never married you. I'd rather have the dream than the man!"

Other titles by

LILIAN PEAKE
IN HARLEQUIN PRESENTS

Other titles by

LILIAN PEAKE
IN HARLEQUIN ROMANCES

LILIAN PEAKE

run for your love

Harlequin Books

TORONTO·LONDON·NEW YORK·AMSTERDAM
SYDNEY·HAMBURG·PARIS·STOCKHOLM

Harlequin Presents edition published February 1980
ISBN 0-373-10341-7

Original hardcover edition published in 1978
by Mills & Boon Limited

CHAPTER ONE

Hesitantly, then decisively, the engine spluttered to a stop. I mustn't panic, Olivia told herself firmly, gripping the steering wheel as if by pretending that all was well the car would move.

The lowering sky held threats of rain, snow and heaven knew what else. It glowered down on the dip and rise of field and fell. Admittedly, it was only the beginning of March—a crazy time of year, people had told her, to go north to visit, for the first time, the dales and hills of England's green and pleasant land.

Crazy it might have been, Olivia had thought, but for the first time in her life, why shouldn't she do something foolish? Those people had not spent ten years of their lives—from mid-teens to mid-twenties—acting as companion to, nurse to, and devoted niece of a somewhat demanding, although always loving aunt.

In vain she turned the ignition key. There was still no response. It had begun to rain. It spattered over the windscreen and ran downwards to the ground. Liquid ... the car won't run on air ... She put a hand to her head. When had she last filled the tank? Hours ago, just after her midday meal in the town many miles back. Why hadn't she thought, why hadn't she realised that there would be no filling station in these wild parts?

Olivia sighed and looked about her. Then she closed her eyes and visualised the tamed splendour of the South Downs, with their criss-cross of well-trodden footpaths and signposted tracks. She opened her eyes. No signposts anywhere in sight, only the desolation of the intimidating magnificence of the limestone landscape surrounding her. Out of nothing came a fear and a foreboding which made her want to scramble out and run.

But where could she run to? No matter in which direction she looked, the moors stretched endlessly. The only other living creatures in sight were the swooping, incurious birds and the totally indifferent sheep, and even they were barely visible, just scattered white specks on the hillsides.

Resigned to the fact that no matter how much she fretted, the car was staying right where it stood, Olivia climbed out. The rain had stopped. She locked the doors and went round to the car boot. From it she hauled a haversack containing a few toilet articles, half a flask of coffee and a small pack of Cream Crackers, which was all she had in the way of food.

The car was in a reasonably safe position. It stood with its wheels off the road on the grass verge where, with a certain presence of mind, she had manoeuvred it on hearing the spluttering of the engine. Apprehensively, Olivia looked about her. Although she had passed only two vehicles inside an hour, she encouraged herself with the thought that before long, some kind of transport must surely come by.

Gritting her teeth, she hung the haversack over her shoulder together with her handbag and started to walk. Darkness came early, hastened by the black cloud-mass looming above, and Olivia acknowledged that her trek had been undertaken more in hope than in confidence of attaining her goal. Since the car had carried her mile upon mile without sight of a filling station, how could she expect her two legs, with their inbuilt human weaknesses, to achieve better results?

At the side of the road there was an ancient milestone. She crouched to read it but was able only to decipher the upper part of its message. 'Three miles to——' The destination had been worn away by the passage of time. She sat on the stone, balancing precariously, to drink the last of the coffee and to nibble the crackers. Then the rain began again.

The hood of her quilted jacket kept her head reasonably dry. Her slacks were made of strong fabric and resisted the lighter raindrops. Her shoes were flat-heeled and comfortable. All that was missing was an end to her journey.

At first she thought the light was an illusion, it seemed so far away. The last glimmerings of rain-soaked daylight revealed that it was to the left of the road and at a lower level. This indicated that it was shining from a building which stood in a hollow, sheltered by the moorland which rose steeply behind it.

While Olivia walked, the distant building took shape. As her steps carried her nearer, her apprehension grew. The rambling nature of the structure and the ruggedness of its surroundings increased that apprehension still more.

When she came across the track which, she calculated, must lead to the source of the light, she slowed to a stop. She had reached a moment of decision. Should she continue, her hopes fading, along the deserted and seemingly endless road? Or should she walk along that track, going wherever it led, finding—who could tell?—a sympathetic welcome, assistance from traditionally warm-hearted country people and, most important of all, warmth and temporary shelter from the relentless rain?

The building beckoned and she could not resist its call. It was a decision which was to alter the whole course of her life.

As she picked her way along the rock-strewn track, she mused about the occupants of that rambling building. Maybe it was a thriving farm—she had driven past quite a few. Maybe she would be greeted by the noise and strong, but healthy, smell of farm animals. There would undoubtedly be the barking of a dog, since every farmer appeared to possess one ...

Yes, there it was, faint at first, growing louder and more insistent the nearer she ventured. There was a gate to the farmyard, but it stood open. There could only be one reason for that. No farmyard gate was fixed in an open position unless there were no animals to escape.

It was plain that at this farm there were no animals. No

welcoming family, either, because' if there were, they would
not have allowed the outbuildings to fall into near-ruin, the
main farmhouse to remain largely windowless, the roof to
decay over their very heads.

She had to face facts. Except for a furiously barking dog,
the place seemed deserted. Then she frowned. No dog,
however clever, could surely reach up and switch on a light,
keep a generator throbbing in a nearby shed and light a
fire from which smoke climbed slowly out of a chimney.

There just had to be someone there! Whoever it was,
however, was deaf to her knock. Had it been too timid, and
were the occupants hard of hearing? Surely they could not
all be deaf, except the dog? The rain fell so heavily it
bounced off the ground, slid over her hood and trickled
round her neck. A determination entered into her to gain
admittance to the unresponsive building, no matter how
heedless of her plight the residents might be.

The knock was louder this time. She banged with her
fists, shouted and waited. It seemed she was carrying on a
very one-sided conversation with the dog, because no one
else reacted to her demand for admittance. Soaked almost
to the skin, Olivia took matters into her own hands. No
matter how large, and whatever breed the dog might be,
she was storming the barricades of that building, even if it
meant climbing in through one of those broken windows.

Quietly she turned the handle. The door was neither
locked nor bolted. It opened—and the dog's barking rose
to a bloodcurdling howl. Breathing deeply, Olivia found it
necessary to make a lightning decision. Should she step
into that room and be savaged to death by a ferocious
animal? Or should she turn and run, only to die of drown-
ing or exposure on the moors, depending on whether the
incessant rain or the biting cold got her first?

A black nose above a furiously working jaw made her
mind up for her. The door was pushed aside and she faced
a snarling canine snout, a long black furry body tensed to
spring and a growling which made her blood run colder
than the weather outside.

From inside the farmhouse came a harsh shout. 'Raff! Be silent, hound!'

The dog stayed as it was, poised for attack, eyes carrying on the verbal fight, daring the intruder to move a step forward. Olivia, heart pounding, held the dog's eyes.

She moistened her lips, whispered, 'Hallo, Raff?' i tentative question. It was as if she had waved a wand. The dog straightened, its tail moved madly, its tongue hung out and it nuzzled the hand that had ventured downward to stroke it.

Olivia nearly fainted with relief. People said dogs knew a friend. Maybe they were right, because here was this animal which, seconds ago, seemed all set to tear her apart, now wrapping himself round her legs and leaping up to rest his paws on her shoulders. As she laughed and stroked the head, she noticed attached to the dog's collar a gold-coloured metal name tag.

It made her catch her breath. Not only did the tag carry a name, it bore a hallmark, which could only mean the tag was gold. With the dog's paws still on her shoulders, she struggled to read the owner's name and address which was engraved on the back of the tag.

'Raff! Down, sit. Sit, boy, do you hear?'

The tag slipped unread from her fingers, the dog lowered himself to the floor. Ears down, tail down, Raff obediently sat. What Olivia saw when she lifted her eyes to look at the newcomer frightened her more than the first impact of the snarling dog.

It was the deep brown eyes of the man which caused that fear, the reckless abandonment in them, the furious disbelief that anyone should have the audacity to invade his fastness, the bitterness in them and finally, the fierce anger.

'What the hell do you want?' It was as if the man were still speaking to his dog, but the brown eyes were on Olivia.

Her lips were stiff with fear, her throat had closed up, her brain in the early stages of petrifaction. His appearance was that of a hermit. His jeans were torn at the knees. His sweater—a pitiful barrier against the cold—was holed at the elbows. His hand was in his trouser pocket. His feet were bare except for sandals.

His hair was long and black. His beard was black, too. He was tall, his shoulders broad. His frame was lean and seemed not to possess a singler layer of spare flesh. His voice was educated. No matter how hard he might try to conceal the fact, the note of refinement lingered. But the look in the eyes remained menacing, the full lips taut and uncompromising.

'I'm—I'm sorry, truly sorry——' Olivia said. 'My car.' She waved her arm vaguely, her sense of direction gone. 'Wouldn't go. Ran out of petrol.'

He looked her over, eyes insolent. 'At least try and be original.' She had pushed back her hood, revealing wide, tired eyes, bedraggled light brown hair, pale, weary oval-shaped face. Her soaked slacks clung to her legs, her shoes squelched with absorbed moisture.

'It's true,' she said faintly. 'It's a little way back. I've been walking, looking for a filling station. I'm not strong enough to push the car.' She looked down at herself in an effort to reinforce her statement. He was not slow in following the path her eyes had taken.

She looked up and caught his expression. Her fear returned and she stepped back, nearer to the door. The dog's ears lifted, his head rose a fraction from the floor.

'Yes,' the man said, eyes glinting, 'I'm a rapist. You should be frightened, madam. I'm a murderer. I'm an escaped prisoner.' She shook her head, but he could not hear the drumbeat of her heart. 'Look at me. I'm capable of killing, aren't I? Who would know, eh?' He moved towards her, but Olivia stood her ground. Her hands went into wet pockets, fists clenched. She swallowed. She did not move.

He stood still. 'Will you get out?'

Again she shook her head, this time in despair. 'I'm soaked, I'm tired, I'm—I'm hungry. Please, Mr——' He was silent. 'I don't care if—if you are a criminal, just let me get dry. You've got a fire somewhere—I saw the smoke. Just give me some water, a dry biscuit. Anything . . .'

'Look, girl, I've got the plague. I've got the evil eye. I'm infectious. I'm contagious. Everything I touch becomes infected. *Now* will you go?'

As if to underline his words, a cough racked his body and he bent double. Olivia thought, He's a good actor ... Then she saw his face. It was so white he looked near to death.

Dear heaven, she thought, he *is* ill. If he really was alone, with no one to look after him, there was no doubting he would not last much longer.

As if he had guessed her thoughts, he rapped, 'Out, get out! What do I have to say, what do I have to do to convince you I'm dangerous? Go, while I let you ...'

Olivia bit a trembling lip, backing towards the door. He did not really frighten her, but she could not stay. It was plain there was nothing she could do to convince *him*, either.

The dog was on his feet, tail working madly, eyes bright. Olivia looked at the creature sadly. He thinks he's going for a walk, she thought, and closed the door on both of them. A furious barking had her standing irresolute. She had disappointed the dog, but pleased the master. Forlornly she pulled her hood into place and, bracing herself, stepped on to the churned-up yard, wincing under the impact of the pelting rain.

In the few minutes in which she had had a roof over her head, a mist had risen, blanketing the grey wilderness and making an alien land seem as desolate as the man who inhabited the decaying farmhouse. A high-pitched howl reached her as she made her way back to the road. She sighed. At least the dog had liked her even if his owner had hated her on sight.

Her end had been decided, not by herself, but by him. She *would* die—not at the hands of a savage dog, but from exposure to the merciless elements. If she walked on along that road, she would get lost in the mist. If she lay down with exhaustion she would probably contract pneumonia, become too weak to walk and slowly fade away ...

A deep-throated barking had her listening intently. It was coming nearer ... Through the mist a form took shape, a black shaggy thing which hurled itself at her legs and jumped all round her feet. Only when she turned to go back to the farmhouse was the dog satisfied, then he raced ahead, turning every few moments to make sure she was following.

The door stood wide. Only a human hand could have opened it. The dog, it seemed, had had the last word. But his name tag had gone.

The black labrador pushed his way in and waited expectantly for Olivia to follow. There was no welcoming party in the form of a dark-eyed, angry man to greet her.

Quietly she closed the door and stood shivering in the unheated room. The ceiling was high and, like the walls, darkened with patches of damp. The carpet underfoot was in places worn threadbare. The wide hearth was empty. A solid wooden table stood in the centre. There was one threadbare armchair.

Once a family must have lived there. Once the room must have echoed with children's laughter, domestic pets must have draped themselves over chairs and carpet—this carpet, perhaps, Olivia thought, looking down.

She was puzzled by the quietness. Where was the man? Where had the dog disappeared to? Her first requirement was to dry her clothes, but in doing so, even if that fire which she knew must be burning somewhere was something that could be shared, with what could she cover herself while her own clothes dried?

Through the door there seemed to be a lobby. Stairs led upwards, but their uncovered treads held no invitation, warning of even worse to come if she ventured to the next floor. A fit of coughing came, not from upstairs, but from another downstairs room. It was a sound which aroused her deepest compassion.

Whether the man was a hermit, a reprobate or even, as he had hinted, a criminal, he needed medical attention. She swung round. She was being watched. In the doorway of a room, the dog sat on his haunches, noting every move she made. Relaxing with relief, she whispered, 'Raff!'

He came to her at once, eyes bright, tail working madly. She crouched down to stroke his coal-black fur and said close to his ear, 'Tell me where he is, Raff. He needs help, Raff, otherwise he'll die. And if he dies, Raff—well, every human life is precious, especially——' She checked herself. What had she been going to say? 'Especially this man's'? What did he mean to her? He was a perfect stranger and one, moreover, who had spoken only harsh, dismissing words to her. So——?

Hurriedly she went on, 'If he died,' she stroked the dog's head, 'you'd be left alone, with no one to care for you.'

'Raff!' It was easy for Olivia to trace the room from which the gruff voice had come. 'Here, dog. For God's sake, hound, don't go over to the enemy!'

Olivia stood unsteadily, watching the dog dart into the room at his master's command. 'Enemy'? How could she be the 'enemy', when she didn't even know the man?

The door stood open, but no more sound came from the room. Olivia crept nervously to the doorway. A bout of shivering took hold of her, and she called softly, 'Please, tell me where the fire is so I can dry myself.'

The silence was so long she wondered if the man had heard. She moved two steps inside. The first thing she saw was a bed. Its sparse covers were rumpled, and there was a dishevelled figure sprawled over it, supine and listless. She noticed that the ragged jeans had gone. Others, in a better state of repair, had taken their place.

The dark eyes which regarded her burned with a feverish energy. 'You can stay the night,' he barked, 'no longer than that.'

'It's all I want. And to get dry. And—and something to eat. I'll pay you. It looks as if you need the money. You could buy yourself——' her glance around showed how many things were wrong, so many that she was unable to mention any particular item. His needs seemed to be so great. 'Buy yourself—things,' she finished weakly.

He half-raised himself on to his right elbow, looking her over insolently. 'You've got so much money, you don't know what else to do with it but give it away to the dregs of society like me?'

Caution made her pause before replying to the cynical

question. She did indeed have some money—the generous amount her mother's sister had left her in her will. Never in her twenty-six years had she been used to a surfeit of money. The thought of owning such a sum had disturbed her peace of mind so much that she had decided to turn her back on the problem for a few weeks. She would leave behind the large house her Aunt Molly had left her which, since the death of her mother eleven years before, had been the only home she had known.

At first, the taste of the new-found freedom had been heady. For the first time in her life she had been free to point to a map of the world and say, 'I'll go there,' and no questions asked. The fact that it had been the north-east of England her finger had pinpointed had been mere chance. Anyway, since she had been no farther north than the city of Birmingham, even a journey to the north-east had excited her.

Despite the cold weather, and the difficulties it presented, something had beckoned her on—and on. Driving through pouring rain with the windscreen wipers working madly, splashing through melting snow as she had driven through unfamiliar country lanes and climbed challengingly steep hills had only added to her sense of anticipation and excitement.

Had she been destined, she wondered, to enter this neglected farmhouse and meet this hostile man? Had some strange force with a strength over which she had no control drawn her there?

All the time she had been thinking, the man had been studying her face, but his hard expression had not changed. He was waiting for an answer to his question and it seemed he would not be content until he received one.

'What makes you think,' she parried, 'I have a small fortune tucked away?' She looked down at herself, teeth chattering. 'Would I——'

'Turn up on my doorstep like a drowned rat?' He relaxed with a sigh of indifference on to his back. 'Who knows? Who knows anything any more?' His eyes closed.

Olivia panicked. Before he slept she must discover where

she could dry her clothes. 'Mr——' She *had* to have a name by which to call him. 'Mr—what?' she asked.

'What's in a name?'

'I've got to call you something.'

'Why?' His eyes narrowed and as his gaze moved over her, it seemed as if he were stripping her bare, layer by layer. 'How long were you planning to stay? There's only one bed, but I might move across and make room for you. I warn you, I'm a little out of practice——'

She jerked her wet hood into place and started to walk out. The dog followed. A burst of coughing racked the man. Raff sat, head on one side, a whining, barking noise coming from his throat. It was as if he were saying, 'Please stay, please stay.'

'Back, hound!' the voice cracked from inside the room. 'Let her go. She's worthless, like all women. We're best alone.'

Olivia felt the chill of her damp clothes strike to the very heart of her. It was no use. She could not launch herself into that strange, eerie outside world until she was better equipped to do so. She walked boldly back into the room.

'Will you please tell me where there's a fire?'

His eyes were closed, his head turned away. He looked frighteningly pale.

'In the grate,' he murmured, 'where else?'

So the only source of warmth was in his room? As she peered round the door, she saw the wisp of smoke curl upwards. It needed stirring back to life. She removed her jacket, looked round for a chair on which to spread it and found one piled with books, so she draped the jacket over those as well.

Underneath she wore a woollen jacket, buttoned high to the neck. That, too, was wet. No use hesitating, it must be dried. Beneath that was a high-necked sweater. This was damp enough to need drying, too. Her slacks still clung, making her legs cold and clammy.

The problem which sprang to her mind seemed insoluble. She needed to uncover herself almost to the skin. She required replacement clothes while her own dried.

'Please, Mr——'

'Delaney,' he said tiredly, 'Mac Delaney.'

'Please, Mr Delaney, I need clothes while mine dry.'

His eyes opened and his head turned slowly. 'Can't you use your own?'

'They're back in my car, in a suitcase.'

He motioned to a cupboard across the room. 'Enough there to cover your modesty. Leftovers from my dubious past before I took to my life of crime.'

He turned on a smile so sinister she had to force herself to remain where she was.

'What the hell are you doing in these parts in this weather, anyway? Has some journal of the gutter press sent you to open up old sores?'

'You're not implying I'm a newspaper reporter?' she asked with astonishment.

'All right, so you're on the level.'

'Yes, I am! If you must know, I'm taking a few weeks off.'

'Off what? Work? What's your work?'

That was difficult. 'I haven't got a job,' she answered slowly.

He lifted himself on to his right elbow again. Strange how his left arm seemed to lie there as if reluctant to move.

'Then why aren't you looking for one, instead of wandering about in these wild places knocking on strange doors, walking into the home of a man as rotten inside and out as the building he inhabits?'

'I—just don't need to work. At present, that is.'

'Good grief,' he sneered, 'you don't mean that I'm entertaining one of your actual upper classes?'

She ran a finger round the damp neck of her sweater. 'Strange as it may seem, considering the circumstances,' she murmured, 'but I would have placed you in that class myself.'

'My God,' he said disgustedly, sinking back, 'how the culture clings!'

Olivia waited for him to continue, but he closed his eyes

again. The cupboard he had indicated revealed an odd selection of clothes. Almost hidden by other garments were the jacket and trousers of a black suit. A formal shirt hung limply. There were a couple of zip-fronted jackets, the good quality of which could not be doubted. On a shelf were one or two sweaters thrown carelessly in. There were also two or three pairs of jeans, almost new.

'Stolen,' he muttered, 'or the pickings from various rummage sales.'

Should she believe him? In the absence of other evidence, she had to. Her hand fastened on to the softness of a pure wool blue sweater. She turned quickly to assure herself his eyes were closed, then she jerked her own sweater over her head, dropped it and checked again. He was watching her, the cynicism narrowing his eyes and twisting the smile on his full lips.

'By heaven,' he muttered, 'just right for ravishing.'

'Will you please close your eyes again, Mr Delaney?' she said, trying to untangle the sweater. 'Will you stop *watching* me? What kind of man are you——?'

'I told you, lady. A rapist, a lecherous swine, a crim——'

'I don't believe you, Mr Delaney,' she said, breathing deeply to steady the erratic beating of her heart.

'Want some proof?' he sneered.

'All right,' she said, feeling the fear increase, 'so you have me at your mercy.' The trembling began and she could not control it. It was a combination of chill, exhaustion and fear. 'But, please,' her eyes filled and she dashed the moisture away, 'will you leave me with some dignity? I d-didn't ask my car to stop. I didn't ask to get caught in this terrible weather. I didn't want to wish my presence on you w-when you so obviously w-want to be left to your solitude . . .'

He sank back, but his eyes did not leave her. As fast as she could manage, she struggled into the blue sweater. It didn't matter that it reached to her thighs, that the sleeves were so long they covered her hands, that the neckline was so high it almost enveloped her chin. It covered her and made her warm and she hugged it to her.

He must, she thought, looking down at herself, have broad shoulders to fill this. He must possess sufficient height to accommodate the high neckline, arms long enough to occupy the sleeves. Arms, she thought, still shivering, and turned to look at him. His eyes were still on her, but in them lurked the look of a man whom fortune had hit unfairly, had dealt with with a ruthless hand. Yes, that left arm lay on the bed while the right arm was raised to support his head.

His brown eyes burned with a brittle bitterness, but there was in their depths a vulnerability which tore at her heart. When she walked away from that farmhouse tomorrow, he would be alone again. What would happen to him then?

CHAPTER TWO

It was no use, she could not bring herself to step out of her soaking slacks under the eyes of this man. She flipped a pair of his jeans from the bar of a coat-hanger and hurried outside. His jeering laughter followed, then she heard, 'Raff, back, dog! Here. Sit.'

So Mac Delaney, as he had called himself, had sufficient refinement and courtesy to respect her desire for privacy on certain occasions. She returned to his room to find him standing near the fire, staring into it. At his hard, brooding expression, she checked her footsteps, but he looked up.

His smile mocked as he saw the picture she presented. His jeans flapped over her feet so that she walked on the hems. The waistband had slid precariously to rest on her hips which were so slim the jeans threatened to slide lower.

'I'm sorry to trouble you,' Olivia said, 'but is there something I could use to fix them into place?'

'Why bother?' he said indolently, moving to sit on the side of the bed.

'Something,' she persisted firmly, 'to hold them up? I don't suppose you possess a belt, but a piece of string——?'

'String. In the kitchen drawer.' As she turned to go, he added, 'You might also find a revolver or two and a flick-knife or two, but don't hold them against me, will you? I'm only a common murderer, after all.'

Olivia pressed her lips together. 'You're as much a murderer, Mr Delaney, as I—Oh!' Out of the corner of her eye she saw an insect scurrying across the floor. It was pure reflex action to reach out with her foot and kill it.

He laughed loudly and stood up. The colour, she noticed, was creeping back into his cheeks. 'Which proves my point, doesn't it?' he commented. 'You're a killer, too. Automatic, like me, only I chase a different sort of victim.' He moved

19

swiftly behind her and her neck was hooked back by his arm—his right arm. She had no choice but to gaze backwards and upwards into his eyes.

Her mouth was dry, her heart hammering like a primitive drumbeat, warning of the approach of warring hordes. There was no doubting the desire to wound in the depths of his gaze. It would not take much, she thought, panicking, to stir it to life. There was cruelty and harshness and a ruthless dismissal of conformity to society's laws.

There was something else—penetration into the deepest caverns of her being. A keen brilliance in his eyes which sought, like a powerful light beam, for undiscovered treasures in the attics of her mind. He was, in appearance, a mysterious, unkempt, hostile man. She was, at that moment, in no position to delve beneath that surface appearance. His hold on her neck tightened and she knew that, no matter what his intentions might be, there was nothing she could do to escape from him.

'Mr Delaney,' she whispered, 'you're hurting me.'

At once he released her and the room spun. In an effort to avoid a faint she crouched low, bending her head. After a few moments the feeling passed and she felt herself being helped across the room. There was only the bed to sit on and its springs gave beneath her.

She tried raising her head and he could not have missed her white face. 'I'm sorry,' she murmured. 'It's not a habit of mine to faint.' Then the shock hit her in the form of nausea, and she rolled sideways on to the bed, pulling up her legs, hugging herself and lying perfectly still.

The man had returned to stand with his back to the fire. When Olivia's eyes fluttered open, she saw that he was watching her with dead eyes. His right hand stroked the softness of his ragged beard. A spasm of coughing shook him and his right hand moved to cover his mouth. He turned to face the dying fire.

Slowly Olivia uncurled and dropped her feet to the floor. It was he who was ill, not herself. Her fright had passed. His illness would not leave him so quickly.

'Mr Delaney,' she said, 'you should be here, in bed.' She

pushed back her light-brown hair, but one or two curls obstinately sprang forward. 'You really should be in hospital. Or at least have someone to look after you.'

He faced her. 'Don't tell me you're offering yourself for hire? If you became my tame housekeeper,' he sneered, 'you'd have to do it for nothing. I've hardly got a penny in the world. And tell me, what woman does *anything* for nothing?'

A pattern was taking shape. It was becoming painfully clear how much he hated women. There must have been one, somewhere, some time, who had caused this catastrophic change in his personality and his way of life. Instinctively Olivia knew that the man she saw now had once been a very different person indeed.

She looked down at the dog who had come to sit in front of her. He lifted his paw and she took it, laughing. 'Raff,' she said, 'oh, Raff!' and she slid from the bed and hugged the dog. 'You're the only living thing with any warmth in this place.' She heard the dog's owner draw a sharp breath and was satisfied. Her words, like a missile, had successfully nosed in on their target. 'I'm hungry, Raff,' she told the animal, 'so hungry I could even eat one of your dog biscuits or gnaw one of the bones you've hidden away in the ground outside.'

There was no reaction from her reluctant host.

'Raff,' Olivia went on, 'where's the food? Where's it kept?' She looked expectantly up at her host.

'Since you've asked my dog,' he said, 'let him give you the answer.'

She straightened quickly. He said with a mocking lift of an eyebrow, 'Stalemate, Miss—er——?'

'Barnes,' she supplied. 'Olivia. And thanks for the advice. Since I rate the dog's intelligence and good sense higher than his master's, I'll go where he leads me.'

'You, Miss Barnes,' was the response, 'will live to regret that statement.'

'I'm glad I'm going to *live*, Mr Delaney.'

'I didn't say for how long, Miss Barnes,' he answered blandly.

She clamped her teeth together, apparently in anger, but in reality to stop them from chattering at the threat in his words. 'Raff,' she said, 'kitchen!' The dog's tail wagged but he did not move.

'Biscuits . . . drink——?' She took a breath and played her last card. 'Walk?'

The dog dived through the door, scampered along a corridor, almost fell down three steps and squatted expectantly in front of a leather leash. Her inspired guess had worked.

'You won't like what you see, Miss Barnes,' Mac Delaney scoffed, calling after her. 'A nicely brought up girl like you will be horror-struck by the state of my kitchen.'

Disappointed at the broken promise, the dog began to bark. Olivia patted his head, then, looking round, put a hand to her own. Mac Delaney was right—she did not like what she saw. Unwashed crockery filled the deep, old-fashioned sink. Saucepans and cutlery covered the unscrubbed wooden draining board. There was the smell of food as though the windows—which, surprisingly, were intact—had not been opened for months.

It was a spacious kitchen, designed for the large families of the time in which the farmhouse was built. There was an ancient electric cooker, an even older refrigerator and, to her surprise, a small washing machine. All the electrical equipment, she assumed, was fed from the generator she had heard working in a nearby shed.

In a corner stood a solid-fuel-burning enclosed fire which, when alight, no doubt heated the water. It was not alight now. Across the kitchen a piece of rope was strung, serving as a crude attempt at an indoor clothes line. A white shirt, of surprisingly good quality, hung from it. It had been joined by three pairs of socks.

The jeans he had lent her began to slide down her hips. She hitched them back into place and searched in two or three drawers before she found the string to which her host had referred. There were no scissors in sight so she doubled the string, slipped it through the loops spanning the waistband and tied it securely. She had a feeling of being watched and glanced up quickly. Mac Delaney was standing on the steps. He came down to kitchen level.

'Food, Miss Barnes, is what you're looking for now,' he drawled from the doorway. He stood, right arm resting against the door frame, smiling at her lost expression.

'Where is it, please?'

'Ask my dog.' His twisted smile, the ragged beard and untidy hair, gave him a satanic look. 'His intelligence is greater than mine, is it not?'

Olivia walked across the room and flung a cupboard door wide. There were tins and packets and boxes enough to withstand a year-long winter. She stared at them, then at her host. 'If you're as poor as you make out,' she challenged, 'how did they get there?'

Hand in his pocket, he strolled towards her. 'I have my methods. Didn't I tell you—I'm a criminal in hiding, Miss Barnes. I rob, I steal, I plunder. I look after my own interests and to hell with the rest of mankind—and especially womankind. I nourish my body, I nurture my bitterness, I feed my hatred, I indulge my appetite.'

His arm caught her waist in a grip of iron, jerking her against him. Only her deep, erratic breathing gave away the hysteria which was rising within her. She looked up into blazing eyes, saw, even in her panic, the classical straightness of his nose, and, where his beard allowed, the sensual fullness of his lips.

A longing arose in her to feel those lips on hers, as intimate and demanding as was the pressure of his body against hers now. It was a feeling so strong it almost swamped the fear. When his right hand left her waist and fastened round her throat, she closed her eyes.

'Yes, Miss Barnes,' he said softly, 'you need to be frightened of me. Even with one hand I could throttle the life out of your body, and who would there be to hear your screams and come to your aid?'

Her eyes fluttered open and she gazed into the depths of his. A flicker passed across them and she held her breath. His hold on her throat slackened, his hand moved to tilt her face upward. The brooding look in his eyes did not lessen her fear.

'Shall I wreak my vengeance on you for what life has done to me? Fate brought you to my doorstep, put you here within my power.' His hand encompassed her neck again, tighter than before. 'Why don't you run, little fool? Why don't you struggle? Why doesn't a look of loathing come into your grey, unfrightened eyes?'

There was the patter of rain on the windows, the hiss of the wind as it crept under ill-fitting doors and rattled broken catches as if it were another occupant of the house. The dog whined at the swaying leash.

The hand around Olivia's neck fell away and her relief was so enormous she collapsed against the man's body, her forehead resting against his chest. For a few seconds she stayed there, waiting for her heart to steady, her pulses to slow to their normal rate. His arms hung at his sides.

She lifted herself from him and turned towards the cupboard, raising her arm and resting her head against the door which had swung closed. When she heard his footsteps taking him away, she remembered that, as her head had rested against him, his heart had also throbbed, with a persistent, primitive drumbeat.

After a while, Olivia felt composed enough to continue her search for food. It occurred to her that she could not sit at that wooden table in the kitchen and eat alone.

As she walked towards the room he occupied she heard a spasm of coughing. Her footsteps quickened. He sounded in distress. When she reached the room he was sprawled exhausted on the bed, his head to one side. His breathing seemed laboured and she moved swiftly to his side.

'Mr Delaney,' she said, 'Mr Delaney.' He did not respond. His face was drained of colour. She pushed his hair from his face and felt the moisture on his forehead. She pulled a paper tissue from the circular table beside the bed. Its pressure absorbed the beads of perspiration as she used it in a stroking motion.

The bedcover had been pushed aside and she pulled it back, arranging it over him as he lay on the blankets. He was so still she thought he must be sleeping, but as she stood looking down at him, her eyes filled with compassion, his opened. Even then there was cynicism in them as they rested on her.

'Why do you bother to try to save the scum of the earth from extinction?'

She continued to look down at him.

'Is it just that it's your vocation? Are you a trained nurse and therefore simply doing your duty?'

'I'm not a trained nurse. I spent ten years looking after an invalid aunt until she died.'

'And,' with a faint, mocking smile, 'are you going to look after me until I die?'

'You're not going to die, Mr Delaney. Maybe if I hadn't come, you would have done, but——'

He was entirely alert now. 'You leave this place tomorrow.' It was an order.

'Don't worry,' she retorted, reproaching herself for presuming that he welcomed her help, 'neither wild horses nor an eager dog will stop me from going tomorrow.'

He pushed aside the cover and swung off the bed.

'Will you lie down again, Mr Delaney?'

'I'll be bossed by no woman.'

He crouched to replenish the fire, stirring it until it flamed. He held out his hand to the warmth.

'What would you like to eat?' Olivia asked.

He straightened to face her. 'Nothing. If I want anything, I can get it myself.'

'But——' Her eyes went to his left arm.

'Don't pity me,' he snapped. 'My car crashed into a wall. Everything that happened afterwards I brought on myself.'

'But,' Olivia said, bewildered, 'all this . . .' indicating the way he lived, 'I don't understand. Why, why?'

'You don't have to understand. You're passing by. Tomorrow you walk out of my life. Now, get out of my room. I don't need you, woman, do you hear?' At his raised voice, Raff came scampering into the room. 'I don't need any living creature. Except my dog.'

When the dog tried to follow Olivia from the room, his

master grasped his collar; then slammed the door with his foot.

Olivia sat in the kitchen staring out of the uncovered window. There was a blackness beyond it which acted as a backdrop to the images which followed each other across her mind like television pictures, never the same for more than a few seconds.

The hard, etched face of a man with eyes which haunted, which challenged and defied the world and had surely known torment and pain ... Which, her intuition told her, had known also, somewhere in his past, inspired joy, an ecstasy beyond her knowledge. Had it been the love of a woman which had touched his face and given it, until he lived out his days, an exultation neither she, nor the majority of his own kind, would ever experience? Or was there something else, more elusive, more sublime, beyond the reach of an ordinary person's field of vision?

Even as he had threatened her, as his hand had gripped her neck, there had been about him a look of distinction which not even his ragged appearance could erase.

How the culture clings! he had muttered. So what was this man who, at every opportunity, threatened her in word and action? Where had he come from? Why was he here? Tomorrow she would be gone. He would have passed out of her life. She would never know the answers to her questions. And she felt a sorrow at the thought which transcended all the sorrows she had ever felt.

With a sigh she looked around the large room. It had been backbreaking work clearing the mess, cleaning, scrubbing on her hands and knees. There had been no further sign of man or dog. She had wandered around in her search for the bathroom. They must have heard her footsteps on the uncovered wooden stairs, but his door had remained shut.

The bathroom was large, the bath possessing four claw-like legs. Over it was an electric water heater operated, no doubt, like the electrical equipment in the kitchen, by the generator outside. For the first time in that long day, hot water ran over her hands and, when she stripped, warmed and cleansed her tired body.

There was only one towel which, she supposed, belonged to Mac Delaney. Since there was nothing else, she used it, hoping it would dry before he needed it again. Her own clothes were shut in his room, so she had no alternative but to pull on his jeans, turning up the legs into enormous hems, and wear his sweater, making deep cuffs at her wrists.

From her handbag she took a comb and ran it through her hair. The mirror showed her a face she did not fully know. It was not really herself who looked back but a stranger with a strained and troubled look, who had been touched by fear and uncertainty—and something else so elusive it was beyond definition.

Holding the rickety banisters, she descended slowly to the lobby. Where should she sleep? She had found no other bed. There was a choice between the kitchen floor and the inhospitable room by which she had first entered the farmhouse.

At least that room possessed an armchair, which was better than the floor. It was half an hour to midnight when at last she curled up in the chair. Her head lowered to rest against the back. She wished she had something with which to cover herself and protect her body from the cold.

She must have drifted in to an uneasy sleep because something woke her. There was the sound of an outer door opening, a scurry of eager feet. A few minutes later she heard a sharp call of 'Raff, in now, boy!' The door closed, footsteps walked, paws clicked on the wooden floor then, with the footsteps, climbed the stairs, slowly, slowly . . .

Olivia drifted into a light sleep. It was impossible to guess how much later it was when the door of the large room swung wide. She opened her eyes and thought at first that it was the force of the wind which still whined through cracks and broken windows—until she saw a tall, bearded figure moving towards her, his dog at his heels.

The dog walked faster and curled beside the chair. The man advanced towards her. It seemed that he was carrying something. With his every step her heartbeats quickened. He stooped.

'Dear heaven,' she thought, 'is he really what he said he was? Has he come to finish what he started earlier? Is this where he—where I . . .'

Slowly his right hand lifted the object he held. Far, far more slowly his left arm began to bend. He moved nearer. Terror dried her mouth, deprived her of the power to breathe. Her fingers moved to press against her mouth, tension contracted every muscle in her body until she nearly cried out with the pain.

A light was on somewhere, lighting the area beyond the room and slanting in through the half-opened door. It revealed the nature of the object which, slowly, laboriously, he lifted and moved towards her. It was a quilted jacket. What did he intend to do with it? In a moment, would there be nothing . . .? She was totally at his mercy. She could not move to save her life.

The coat lowered, down, down—*and he was covering her with it to keep out the cold!* In the semi-darkness their eyes met. She knew that her terror had been so great it still lingered in her eyes. In his was a hard, cynical gleam, as if her fear had amused yet annoyed him. Her relief was so great, her gratitude at his thoughtful action so sincere that a smile curved her lips and illuminated her eyes.

'Thank you, Mr Delaney,' she whispered. 'You're very kind.' He did not reply.

He called to the dog who had curled beside Olivia's chair, but the animal did not move. He called again, with the same result. 'Traitor,' he murmured, and the dog yawned and waved his tail. His master went from the room. The door closed, but did not click shut. It was no doubt a hint to the dog that if he changed his mind and sought his master's room as usual, he knew where to find him.

As Olivia slipped into a deep and strangely happy sleep, she remembered how Mac Delaney had moved his left arm for the first time since she had arrived—the first time for who knew how long? He had bent it, and used it, despite the considerable pain he must have felt in doing so. Instinctively she knew that the action had for him been an achievement and the thought pleased her beyond imagination.

When she woke it was morning, but only the hands of her watch gave evidence to prove it. The mist, instead of clearing, had thickened overnight. In fact, the weather was worse than when she had arrived. And this was the morning she had been told to leave!

Uncurling her cramped limbs and stretching them painfully, she pushed her shoulder-length hair from her face. The dog had gone and the door stood wide, indicating that he had nosed it open. Her face felt stiff with the need for washing.

In the bathroom the water heater came to life and very soon she was washing in hot water and looking for a towel. Beside the blue one she had used the night before hung a striped towel, clean and fresh-smelling. Using it and delighting in the way its roughness brought her circulation to life, she could hardly believe that Mac Delaney had taken the trouble to provide her with a towel of her own—unless he had disliked the idea of her using his.

As she descended the stairs and entered the kitchen, the warmth from the solid-fuel boiler told her that her host had been there before her. He had cleared away the ashes and put a match to the fire. The clothes had gone from the line and on the table were her slacks, cardigan, sweater and jacket. On top of the pile was a note.

'Help yourself to food. Thank you for cleaning my kitchen. Goodbye. M.D.'

Olivia trudged along the road, smelling the mist and tasting it. Its hovering dampness was making her almost as wet as the rain the day before. Her haversack and shoulder bag swung lightly at her side. Her heart was as heavy as her footsteps.

She was fighting a feeling of desolation as dense as the mist around her. While she had breakfasted and collected some food to sustain her on her long walk, there had been no sign of her host. Only the dog had scampered into the kitchen to greet her. Then he had sat expectantly at the kitchen door waiting to be let out.

Olivia had let him in again and had received yet another welcome, after which he had sat compliantly while she dried his paws on an old towel which hung on the door. At least, she thought ruefully, the dog of the house accepts me as 'belonging', even if the host of the house doesn't!

Intermittent coughing had told her that Mac was awake. The closed door told her, just as clearly, that he did not wish to see her. It had torn at her heart to leave him when he was in such need of attention. After all, she had rationalised hastily, he was another human being. Compassion, plus her ten years of nursing her invalid aunt, had implanted in her the instinct to go to the aid of anyone in distress, whether stranger or friend.

When she had closed the farmhouse door behind her, shutting in a whining dog, there had been no other reason, she had argued vehemently, for the tug at her very heart-strings at leaving it all behind. It was because her heart was heavy and because the mist was almost choking her that it took her so long to cover the distance to the nearest village.

It was, she discovered later, less than three miles from the farmhouse. She found a general store and post office, an inn, a newsagent and, surprisingly, a hairdresser's shop. Having bought a carton of milk, and cheese to eat with the rolls which she had brought from the farmhouse, Olivia told the storekeeper about her stranded car. He was sympathetic. The only thing he could think of, he said, was to ask one of the local farmers to tow her car behind a tractor to the nearest filling station. That was a good seven miles along the road, he added.

'And you won't get a farmer out in this weather, miss, not on a job like that. Too busy with their own problems in this kind of weather.'

'How long will this fog last, do you think?' Olivia asked.

The storekeeper shrugged. 'Could be gone by tomorrow, or could hang about for days. You on holiday, miss?' he asked. When she nodded, he said, 'Funny time o' year to have a holiday in these parts, isn't it?'

She said noncommittally, 'It just happened that way.'
While he attended to another customer, Olivia wandered
round. When the woman had gone, Olivia asked the man if
there was a bus which came to the village.

'Three times a week,' he told her. 'And today's not one of
them.' He smiled sympathetically. 'Just not your day, is it,
miss?'

She shook her head, hesitated, then said, 'As I came
along, I noticed a—a farmhouse along a track. From the
road, it looked derelict, but—er—there was a light. Do you
know who lives there?'

The storekeeper pulled a face. 'It's derelict all right, miss.
Atherley's Farm. A family called Atherley lived there once.
Born and bred in these parts, they were, all of them. But
one by one they either moved away or died, and then there
was only the old father living there. He just upped and
went—to live with his brother, he said. Gave most of the
furniture away, just left what nobody else wanted.'

'But the light I saw,' she persisted. 'There must be somebody there?'

'That's true. A man came along, let's see, getting on for
a year, now. He moved in. He must have made enquiries
about who it belonged to, found out it was just standing
there rotting, bought it, and made it his home. We don't
see much of him. Keeps himself to himself. All he's got, far
as we can see, is his dog. He's rude to anyone who tries to
get friendly, so we just keep away. I should keep clear of
that place, miss, if I were you.'

Olivia nodded as if she understood and went to the door.

'When the weather clears,' the storekeeper said, 'I'll see
what I can do about your car. If you want putting up for a
few days, I expect old Jim Selby can offer you a room at the
Jug and Bottle over there.'

'Thanks,' said Olivia, 'but I'll have to go back to my car
to get my things.'

The storekeeper nodded and wished her luck. The shop
bell rang above her head and she went out into the wall of
thickening fog. There was a return of the curious feeling of

apprehension she had felt the day before and she knew that she would need a great deal of that thing called luck in the weeks that stretched ahead.

Olivia ate her rolls and cheese sitting in the bus shelter opposite the Jug and Bottle. No other person joined her because, as the storekeeper had said, it was not the day for the bus.

She was too dejected to make plans. Her thoughts wandered aimlessly as if caught up in the heavy mist which enveloped every object in sight. She digested it with her food, she drank it with her milk. It crept into her eyes and filled her nostrils. She liked neither its taste nor its smell.

A sigh came involuntarily as she gazed at the Jug and Bottle. In the summer, no doubt it looked delightful with the window boxes filled with scarlet geraniums. At the moment, it looked what it was—solid, grey and with a durability as long-lasting as the age-old stone with which it had been constructed.

There was no harm, she decided, packing her haversack, in seeing what the place had to offer in the way of accommodation. The proprietor opened the door, a once-white apron round his waist, a harassed look on his face.

Olivia asked if he had a room to let. Bed and breakfast for a few days, that was all she wanted. He rubbed the back of his head agitatedly. 'It's always been my proud boast,' he said, 'that I never turn anyone away. But for the first time ever—you see, miss, I'm in such a state I just couldn't take anyone, not even a stray dog. It's my wife that does that side of it and she's laid up with the 'flu. So's my daughter, who helps her. And, to be honest, I don't feel so good myself. But someone's got to be behind the bar at opening time and since there's no one else, that'll have to be me. So,' he shook his head, 'this time it's got to be "no". Sorry, miss.'

Olivia said she quite understood and turned away dispiritedly. 'Maybe one of the villagers would help out,' the innkeeper called. 'Sometimes in the summer they do bed and breakfast.'

She raised her hand and thanked him and returned to the

bus shelter. It was there, ten minutes later, that she decided to return to her car. At least it would be somewhere to sit. She could listen to the radio and even get out her sleeping bag which she had had the foresight to bring with her in case she wanted at any time to garage her car and walk across the moors to stay for a few nights at a youth hostel. She looked around her as she plodded wearily back along the winding country road and knew that there would be no walking over the moors in that weather.

It seemed hours before she reached a farm gate which she recognised as being near to the track which led to the farmhouse. She kept her head averted, but even if she hadn't there would have been nothing to see. The building was lost in the mist.

Her car was exactly where she had left it. At that moment it seemed a haven. She slid into the driving seat and turned on the car radio, only to discover that she had no patience to spare for the world's problems when she had so many of her own. Nor did she feel in the mood for the kind of music which came from the radio, the relentlessly lively banter of the broadcasters, the loving dedications from one member of a family to another, from a girl to her man, her own true love.

A face formed before her eyes—two intense, deeply brown eyes topped by thick, dark eyebrows. The high-boned facial structure, the full lips, the rounded chin . . . All possessing, under the hard cynicism which time had grafted over the features, an elusive, indefinable sensitivity . . .

Tears rose in her throat, trembled on her lips, welled into her eyes. Why was she crying, she wondered, when she would never see him again, knew nothing of the man's real identity, did not even know whether he really was the criminal he had told her repeatedly—and tried forcefully to demonstrate—that he was?

Drying her tears, she stared at the fog which cocooned the car. She did have a choice. She did not have to stay where she was. If she could find the courage, she could ask his permission to stay at the farmhouse for a night or two longer. There was surely no harm in just walking that way?

Locking the car, she retraced her steps. The mist cloaked every object, silenced every sound. But it did not, it seemed, hide her scent. As she saw the track to the farmhouse opening out to her left, she also saw something else —a bedraggled black shape sitting on its haunches, waiting.

'Raff, oh Raff!' she cried, and ran towards him.

The dog did not venture beyond the track's end. It seemed he had been well trained. He barked, he howled, he barked again. He wagged not only his tail but his whole body. He greeted her as if she had been away for a year.

She caught at his collar and led him to the car to get her suitcase and sleeping bag. He nosed in the boot while she collected other items she might need. The sight of Raff had brought her to a decision. She did not care if his master refused her entry or, with his one strong arm, physically threw her out. If she did not even attempt to return, she would never forgive herself for the whole of her life.

Together they trailed down the track, two damp, dishevelled objects, making for a single door. Inside that door, for one of them a welcome would be waiting. For the other . . .? Olivia tried to steady her heartbeats, but they defied her control and beat even faster. Soon she would know the answer to her question.

A man appeared at the door, catching the dog by the collar. Together they formed a formidable barrier. Olivia put down her case and pushed back her hood. She pressed her lips together to hide her fear.

'I've come back, Mr Delaney,' she whispered.

Mac Delaney made no move to allow her to enter. The dog strained forward, whining and yelping alternately. Despite his great strength, his owner's strength seemed greater. He was not even unbalanced by the dog's efforts.

At last he spoke. 'If I refuse to let you in, my dog would come after you. And then I'd really be alone.'

Was she, for the second time that day, being turned away from shelter? She would keep her dignity and go of her own accord. Her case seemed much heavier as she retrieved it from the soaking earth and swung round, putting the house behind her.

Raff's yelping changed into a frantic barking. He must have broken free because he appeared in front of her, leaping from side to side in an effort to cut off her retreat.

'Raff,' she said, her voice wavering, 'I've got to go. Your master says——'

'He says,' a voice said behind her, 'come in, Olivia.'

CHAPTER THREE

THE door creaked shut. Raff scampered away. The sleeping bag and haversack joined the suitcase on the floor, and Olivia's jacket, saturated by mist and damp, slipped from her shoulders.

Her eyes lifted to meet those of her host and in their depths she saw an enigma that defied solution. He looked down at her strangely, as if he saw, yet did not see her standing before him. Whatever it was that held his thoughts in bondage communicated itself to her also. It was as if she had joined him on another mental plane, on territory so unfamiliar she felt she must reach out and touch him for security and confidence.

As if it possessed a mind of its own, her right hand came out. 'Th-thank you, Mr Delaney, for letting me stay.'

His right hand did not stir to meet hers. She bit into her lower lip to override the pain of being rejected—until she noticed his left hand moving slowly, slowly upwards. She saw him grit his teeth to help him bear the agony of bending his arm, and felt his left hand seek her right hand, gripping it until she almost winced. His hard, cold face was lit by a fleeting smile, like a man who had staked his all on a desperate gamble—and won.

He did not let her go. She felt herself impelled towards him and because he used his left arm—so badly injured in the car accident it seemed to be of little use to him now—she could not bring herself to resist. He still looked ill, more so perhaps than when she had seen him for the last time, as she had thought, the night before. His face had grown more gaunt, his eyes more shadowed, as if sleep had not eased his limbs and tortured mind for many nights.

When he had pulled her so close that their bodies touched, he whispered, 'Warm me, girl out of the mist. Let your warmth creep into me and bring me back to life. I've lost so many things—a woman, a whole world, so much you couldn't even guess.'

Her heart which, at his words, had struggled to a pinnacle, tumbled and bumped to the foot of the mountain. A *woman, a whole world lost*, he'd said. His woman and his lover, perhaps, who, on seeing his injuries, had left him for ever, and he had never forgiven her nor, even against his will, forgotten his love for her.

Tears of compassion rose within her. Her hands lifted to his shoulders to offer him comfort and assurance. She gazed again into his eyes and found that, despite his whispered words, the enigma in them remained. Her lips parted to show small white teeth but even so, when his lips descended and held hers fast, his right arm catching her up and jerking her even closer, she did not understand the ferocity of his action.

Nor could she understand the foolishness of her own emotions—the way they lifted her high to that same pinnacle once more. Hadn't they learnt their lesson? Hadn't they just picked themselves up from a devastating fall? Wasn't he merely using her, simply because she was there, to alleviate his grief at losing the woman he had apparently adored?

Yet she not only allowed but returned the kiss. It seemed to have no end. It was as if he were slaking an unendurable thirst. She responded and yielded and did not refuse when he came back for more, nor when his hand traced out the unexplored and entirely feminine areas of her body.

When he threw her from him so hard she staggered and nearly fell, she was bewildered. 'My God,' he grated, 'I don't want your pity!'

Pity? How could he have interpreted so incorrectly her compliance and submission to his approaches? She shook her head, saying 'But I——' How should she continue—'I want you to touch me, to kiss me,' when until those past few minutes she had not even known it herself? Somehow she must prove to him that she was not the easy game he thought her to be.

'Don't worry,' she responded, trying to assuage her own

hurt by hurting him in return, 'it wasn't pity that let you kiss me. It was just—just a new experience. And,' ignoring his derisive smile, 'it wasn't pity that brought me back here, it was sheer necessity. The inn in the village couldn't take me. I couldn't sleep in my car, so I had no choice but to return.'

With her outburst, her anger died. She remembered his whispered words. *Warm me, let your warmth creep into me and bring me back to life ... I've lost so many things ...* And hadn't he used his injured arm, and hadn't he rejoiced at his achievement?

'I'm sorry,' she said.

He did not ask her why, nor did her apology do anything to help. It had seemed only to reinforce his theory that she had acquiesced to his kiss through pity. His eyes had turned hard again, his jaw had grown rigid and formidable. He turned abruptly and went away. Seconds afterwards, his door closed.

Confused by events piling one on the other, Olivia looked around, feeling lost. Should she make this room hers, or was there a bedroom upstairs in a reasonable enough state to be used? Her eyes drew back at the brilliant lick of flames in the grate. Someone had lit the fire. Since it could not have been the dog, she thought with a smile, it could only have been his master.

She recalled how, when she had first arrived there—was it only yesterday?—there had been only one fire burning and that was in his room. Yet this morning the fire had been burning in the kitchen and now, in here!

From the inner lobby, she could see that his door was still shut. She crept up the stairs and washed in the bathroom, using the towel she had found waiting for her that morning. He hadn't removed it. The fire, the towel ... It was almost as if he had been expecting her back.

There seemed to be six bedrooms. One by one she went into them. Five were bare to the floorboards. The sixth door was locked. No matter how she pushed and turned the handle, it would not open. Fear zigzagged through her. Her doubts returned, hitting her with storm force. Where was the key? Why was it locked? What was inside? Was he indeed a man to be feared?

There was a noise behind her and she almost screamed. Mac Delaney must have crept up the stairs—or had she been so deafened by her ridiculous conjectures she had not heard him? He towered over her, hand in pocket, hair pushed back to reveal a burning forehead.

'What fantasies are you weaving, Miss Barnes?' he asked jeeringly. 'What terrible happenings are you dreaming up that take place behind that locked door?'

There was a note in his voice that might have been anger —or a simmering cruelty. He took a handful of her hair, twisted it and with it impelled her against him. His eyes burned with a feverish brilliance. 'I keep the tools of my trade in that room, Miss Barnes,' he rasped. 'My weapons of destruction, the loot which I take from my victims, the disguises I assume when I go secretly about my evil business. What do you think I have in mind to do to you, my prowling visitor?'

'But——' she choked as he jerked back her head.

'No, my dog wouldn't come to your aid. You see, I lock him in the kitchen.'

'D-don't be silly, I d-don't believe——'

'Oh, but you do, don't you? You don't know what to think of me. I live like a hermit in a broken-down building. I dress in clothes which would disgrace a tramp. What did they tell you about me down in the village? That you shouldn't come near this place at any price?'

Olivia tried to shake her head, but it was too painful. 'You're—you're hurting me, Mr Delaney.' She could not stop the tears which sprang involuntarily as he tightened his hold at her complaint.

'What do I care if I hurt you? You're just another woman. They're all the same—traitors, schemers, parasites. The more you give them, the more they want. They take and give nothing back. They bleed you dry of everything you've got—emotions, feelings, possessions. Then they——'

'It's not t——' she began, but her words were cut off by his mouth.

It was a brutal, consuming kiss, of a kind she had never before experienced. She forgot the pain his hand was inflicting, she was not even conscious of the tears which ran down her cheeks. She gave herself up entirely to the passion —cold and calculated though it was—with which his lips imprisoned hers, to the burning but entirely controlled ardour.

Her arms crept up to his neck and clung. Her body responded in a way which was entirely alien to her, revealing to her sides of her own nature she had not even encountered until now. Slowly she became conscious of what was happening between them and she recoiled, struggling free, hating herself for the encouragement she realised she was giving him.

'What do you think you're doing?' she demanded, backing away and attempting to put the blame for the situation on to him.

'Taking whatever I can get whenever it's offered to me,' he sneered. 'I live a lonely life, empty of all the pleasures of the flesh. My withdrawal from society was voluntary and my solitude self-imposed. But despite my injury,' he indicated his arm, 'I remain a fully-functional male animal. So when a woman walks herself into my lair as you've done —twice—I seize every possible chance of indulging my masculine needs. Can you blame me? Especially as my *guest* is so willing to please.'

With the back of her hand she dried the remains of the tears from her cheeks, then rubbed her hair where his remorseless pulling of it still throbbed.

'I certainly wasn't *eager*,' she flung back. 'How could I be when you were so—so barbaric in the way you kissed?'

'My God,' was his comment, 'you really must be inexperienced!' She felt as immature as a child.

'I thought men were tender when they wanted to please a woman,' she went on, unconsciously revealing how accurate his assumption had been. 'But you didn't want to please me, did you? All you wanted was to satisfy your frustrated desires.'

'True,' he said with a callous smile.

'I know one thing,' she hit back. 'When—and if—I ever marry, the man I choose won't treat me like a robot as you've done. When we make love, it will be with consideration and sensitivity and—and tenderness. But you wouldn't know about them, would you, because you don't possess one single particle of those qualities in your entire personality.'

'You know nothing about me, woman,' he said curtly.

His breathing seemed laboured and she thought it was the anger her words had aroused—until she saw the beads of moisture standing out on his forehead. He pressed the back of his hand to them, found a handkerchief and pressed it against his upper lip.

It seemed he had a fever, as she had suspected. The cough—it racked his body again—his weakness, his burning face, added up inevitably to neglected illness. There was 'flu in the village. Despite his isolation, he must somehow have caught it, perhaps when he had been shopping.

He should be in bed, she thought. He went past her to the bathroom and she ran down the stairs. Raff came to greet her and together they went into the empty bedroom. With a swiftness born of experience Olivia smoothed and tidied the bed.

Mac came into the room and looked at her coldly. He did not thank her. 'I don't need a nurse.'

'I'd do the same for any human being in need,' she retorted. 'You're ill. You should be in this bed.'

'I'll do what the hell I like. Now, will you get out?'

'Your room or the house?'

'Please yourself.' Their eyes clashed. His were dull, hers defiant.

'All right, I will.' As she went from the room, Raff followed and his owner made no attempt to call him back.

It was dark and still the mist did not relent. Through cracks and broken panes of glass, it seeped into the kitchen where Olivia sat huddled over the fire.

The dog lay beside her. He seemed to be the only contented one in the house. She had eaten an evening meal which was little more in size and nutritional value than her meagre lunch. She simply wasn't hungry.

Before she prepared it, she had made some attempt to contact her host, but all her attempts to get a reply had failed. It worried her because it meant he was taking no nourishment. Even soup would have been better than nothing.

For nearly three hours she waited for some sign of life, but there was not even a cough to reassure her. Quietly the transistor radio she had brought with her played at her side, classical music, the kind she preferred. But instead of listening, she found herself straining to catch any sound of movement from Mac's bedroom.

At last she gave in and prepared for bed, washing in the cold bathroom, changing into the pyjamas taken from her suitcase, then pushing her feet into sheepskin-lined moccasins.

Downstairs she unrolled her sleeping bag, folding a sweater to use as a pillow. From the lobby she heard a whining and a sharp bark. It seemed that Raff had grown tired of waiting for his master's call and was himself doing the calling. Fearful that Raff might disturb him, Olivia hurried out to stroke the dog, but he would not be comforted. He was determined to gain admittance to that bedroom.

Holding her breath, Olivia turned the handle. The door creaked on its rusty hinges. She grasped Raff's collar to prevent him from rushing in and together they moved into the room. Raff nosed round the worn slippers at the side of the bed, rested his paws on the bedclothes and licked the lifeless left hand. Then, as Olivia watched him, scarcely breathing, he settled down in front of the fireplace.

Concerned now, she went to the bedside. What she saw made her heart pound. Mac was perspiring so much the shirt he had pulled on but had not buttoned clung to his skin. His forehead was on fire. Olivia had reason once again to feel thankful for the knowledge she had gained in nursing her ailing aunt.

She hurried to the kitchen and found a basin which she

filled with water. There was no suitable cloth to be seen, so she ran upstairs and took her own face-cloth from the bathroom. She hurried down and carried the water into the bedroom, placing it on the table beside the bed. With a hammering heart she lifted the dampened cloth to Mac's forehead, sponging the burning skin.

When his head turned sideways on the pillow, she held her breath. If he woke now, he would tell her to leave him alone. He did not wake. For a few seconds she gazed at his neck and chest. From the point of view of convention, they were out of bounds to her. As a nurse, she knew where her duty lay. Gently she ran the cloth round his neck. Wetting the cloth again, she ran it across the broad expanse of his chest.

A towel lay across a chair. She took it up and soaked up the moisture, stroking the mass of hair until it was dry. His shirt still clung and she knew it must be changed. He wore pyjama trousers, but there was nothing she could do about those. In the cupboard she had seen two or three shirts carelessly folded. She chose one and discovered to her astonishment that it bore the name of a famous maker and that the material was silk.

She gazed at the restless figure and felt compassion stir within her. With her eyes she traced the line of his eyebrows, his hard jaw and tantalising lips. What would it be like to be spoken to by those lips in a kindly way, kissed by them with tenderness and love? She shook away such thoughts and, seizing her courage by its collar before it made its getaway, she put her hands on his shoulder and right arm.

Rolling him on to his side, she slipped off the damp shirt, replacing it with the clean one. She eased him back and ran round the bed to roll him the other way, freeing the soiled shirt. There was scar tissue on the arm, telling of injury and operations but plainly bringing only partial healing.

She urged on the clean shirt, leaning across him to fasten the buttons. She caught the male scent of him, and was trapped by his magnetism, which, even at the height of his fever, reached out and ensnared her. Her hand moved to stroke his hair away from his cheeks and he moved restlessly beneath her touch. Fiercely she bit her lip, expecting the dark eyes to open and dismiss her. They remained closed. He was too tightly enmeshed by the fever to surface to full consciousness.

If she could manage to lift him sufficiently for him to drink, she could dissolve some tablets designed to reduce the fever and coax the liquid into him without his even knowing. She ran from the room and raked in her suitcase, finding the tablets. In the kitchen she half-filled a glass with water and watched the tablets dissolve.

It was more difficult lifting him than she had guessed. With all her strength she eased him up sufficiently high to prevent the liquid from running uselessly away. His eyes fluttered open but, although they settled on her, they did not appear to focus. However, he did nothing to hinder her efforts.

All his barriers were down, eroded to nothing by weakness. Wiping his mouth with a tissue, she lowered him back against the pillows and sighed with relief. Surely he would begin to improve now and the fever start to ebb?

As she looked at his burning face and saw the small, restless movements of his hands—as if he were flexing the muscles of his fingers, even those of his left hand, for action —she knew she would not be able to sleep for worrying. Even if she left him, she would find herself returning constantly to reassure herself about him.

There was a small space on his bed. If she could curl up there, dressed as she was in her robe, even if she slept she would be aware at once of his slightest need and be on hand to attend to it. Again she considered convention and again she dismissed it. There was no one to see her lying beside him, no one to condemn her for being promiscuous and improper. Even Mac Delaney himself would probably never know she had spent the night beside him, since she would be up and about before he woke.

Throughout the night Olivia hardly slept. Frequently she was beside him, bowl in hand, sponging his face and chest.

Once she stood there, having dried him, looking at the breadth of his shoulders, the sensitivity in his features which she had, apparently quite wrongly, accused him of lacking. She replaced the covers over him and his eyes came open. Although they stared at her, she had the chilling feeling that he was still not seeing her. As she watched, his arm, his left arm, began to lift. His left hand came slowly down to cover hers, which still held the blankets.

'Don't leave me now,' his lips whispered. A long pause as his eyes closed. 'You don't know me as I really am,' he went on at last. 'When you walked away, part of me died . . . Knew there must have been someone in the past . . . but not now, not to take you from me when I needed . . .' His hand slipped from hers as he lapsed into silence.

For a long time she looked down at him. To her dismay she found that her lips were trembling. The woman he had lost . . . He had never forgotten her. Even now he loved her so much she haunted his fevered dreams. So why was she upset? The man was a stranger, just as she was a stranger to him. Any feelings she might have developed for him must be denied with all her will power. Alone he might be, but his heart still belonged, probably always would belong, to the woman who had so brutally left him.

Later in the night she managed to persuade him to take more water and tablets. As daylight crept across the room, she went to the window, pushing the curtain aside. The sight that greeted her made her draw a sharp breath. Moorland stretched into the distance, green on the valley floor and rising to a line of grey limestone hills behind the farmhouse. The trees were few in number. Dry stone walls separated pastures on the flatter land, while the fells rose, ridged and peaked and grooved, towards the skyline.

The mist had gone.

Olivia lay on her side facing the man beside her. As the light increased, she saw how his fever had ebbed, leaving him pale and exhausted. He slept a natural sleep. He was getting better.

She pulled the covers over her, closed her eyes and surrendered to her own exhaustion. When she woke she found she was alone, and she sat up, alarmed. Where had he gone? She listened intently and heard water flowing. Whether it was advisable or not, he was taking a bath. A heavy object made the bed sag and she returned to consciousness again with a start.

When paws trampled over her legs and a cold nose touched her cheeks, she squealed and hid her face in the pillow, laughing at Raff's antics.

'Off the bed, hound!' his master snapped, and at once the dog obeyed. He crept away into the kitchen. Since his master seemed to be in an unpleasant mood, Olivia could not blame the dog for getting out of his way. She rolled on to her back and looked up uncertainly at her host. Confused, embarrassed, tongue-tied and filled with self-reproach, she wished she could have followed Raff's example.

Mac Delaney held on to the chair as if to steady himself. His body might be weak, but Olivia could see by his eyes that his mind did not suffer from the same disadvantage. His gaze was so cynical, his look so insolent she stiffened with indignation.

He looked at the basin of water with the face cloth immersed in it. He saw the bottle containing soluble tablets and the glass. He looked at the discarded shirt on the floor, then at the shirt he was wearing. In place of his pyjama trousers he had pulled on jeans. His hair and beard had been combed. Neater and more alert, he looked even more of a stranger.

'So, my little Florence Nightingale, you nursed your patient through the night and brought him back to health.'

She sat up, pushing away her tousled hair and pulling her robe closer round her. 'You're still not completely fit. You should be in bed.'

He gave her a long, considering look. 'Right. I agree to that suggestion—but only if you stay in bed with me.'

'Don't be silly. I—you—I'm not——' Her confusion increased. 'I was only in here to keep an eye on you. After getting up and taking care of you all night, I—well, I was so exhausted I went to sleep.' She avoided his eyes. 'How could I look after you, sleeping in another room?'

With his right hand he buttoned his shirt. 'Tell me something, Miss Barnes. Exactly why did you look after me?'

She hugged her knees, resting her cheek on them. How could she answer him when she did not know the answer herself? 'Because——' For a long moment she thought, then she shrugged. 'Instinct, maybe. My years of conditioning through nursing my aunt.' She stole a glance at him. He still did not seem satisfied. 'Hating to see a fellow human being in distress. My—my womanly inclinations to heal and give comfort.'

Her lips stopped speaking but her thoughts went on. A certain feeling I've got deep down where you're concerned ... The tremendous attraction you have for me ... The magnet you possess which drew me back here even though I might, with an effort, have found other accommodation ...

She didn't believe in love at first sight, but if she had, was that how she might have explained this unaccountable sensation she experienced every time their eyes met? The cry of pain inside her when she had heard him talking feverishly about the woman he had lost? The worry which had kept her awake and alert all night until the dawn showed that his illness was receding?

Again she glanced at him and found a tormenting smile flickering round his mouth. It faded quickly as if the effort had been too much.

'Maybe you're right,' he said with an exasperated sigh. 'Maybe I'm not as fit as I thought.' He dropped on to the bed and lay full length.

'Of course you're not. How could you be when you spent three quarters of the night burning with fever and tossing and turning and muttering——' She stopped, wishing she had been more careful.

His head turned slowly. His eyes held no expression. 'About what—whom—did I "mutter"?'

She lifted her shoulders as if it had been trivial. 'Some woman. It seems you didn't want her to leave you.'

He considered her reply then asked tersely, 'Did I mention a name?'

'No name.' Her cheek found her knees again. 'It sounded as though that woman meant an awful lot to you. I don't know how you can still have any feelings for her after what happened.'

'Oh? And what did happen?'

She grew uncertain at his strange tone of voice. 'Well, judging by what you told me yesterday, the way she walked off and left you after you had been badly hurt in a car accident.'

'I see.' His head sank back to the pillow.

He was silent for so long, Olivia sighed and swung her legs to the floor. His right hand came out, pulling her back so that she was forced to return her legs to the bed. 'Just a moment.' His hand slipped to her wrist and grasped it. If she had not clenched her teeth, she would have cried out at the tightness of his hold.

'Olivia Barnes,' he said, 'will you marry me?'

His body was still, except for the faint rise and fall of his chest. Even his eyes were locked with hers, ensnaring them until she responded one way or the other.

Olivia could not answer. She could only look at the hand on her wrist. 'Please, Mac,' she said, 'you're hurting me.' Always Mac Delaney was hurting her. He followed her eyes and immediately his hold loosened.

Still she could not reply to his question.

'Is there,' he asked, 'somewhere in your life, a boyfriend? One you're serious about?' She shook her head. He closed his eyes as if he needed to concentrate. 'Have you parents?'

'My mother died some years ago. Their marriage had already started to break up. My father remarried, and I hardly ever see him. There was only my aunt. She never married. She was ill on and off for ten years, so I left school at sixteen and looked after her for that ten years. Recently she died.'

'Which left you free?' She nodded. 'Hence this vacation

which brought you to my doorstep?' Again she nodded. 'So you have no ties. Why don't you answer my question?'

'How can I marry you? There's——' she took a breath, 'there's no love between us.' He made a contemptuous, dismissive sound. 'And I only met you yesterday. You're really a complete stranger.'

'Hardly. You spent the night nursing me.'

'I only did what any woman would do.'

Momentarily his eyes hardened. 'Did you?' His voice was dull, disbelieving. 'You slept by my side. You wouldn't leave me. How can you call me a stranger?'

'Oh, Mac, I know nothing about you. Except all the terrible things you've told me.' She waited breathlessly for him to deny all his previous statements about himself. She waited in vain.

He indicated his left arm. 'Is it this that repels you? Does it make you think I'll be useless as a husband? Let me show my little wanderer just how expertly I can make love with only one good arm.'

He rolled on to his side and over again, pushing away her robe and putting his lips to her throat and across her shoulders, trailing a burning line to the base of the deep neckline of her pyjama top. His fingers felt for the buttons, but she clapped her hands over his hand, pushing it away.

'Let me think,' she said urgently, fighting the alien longings he had begun yet again to arouse. 'Just let me think. I know how—how you kiss——'

He rolled on to his back again. 'And I, my Olivia, know how you respond to my kisses. A new experience, you called them. Is your experience of love, I wonder, as extensive as you would like me to believe?'

She was silent for some time, then she said dully, 'I've had no experience of "love" at all, not in the sense you mean.' He was as silent as she had been. 'Does that put you off me?' she asked acidly. 'Would you have preferred some experience in the woman you marry, if only to add spice to the kind of intimate relationship which I'm sure wouldn't be new to you?'

He smiled provocatively. 'Maybe your "purity" will itself

be the spice I need. Maybe it will give new life to my palate which you seem to think has been "dulled" by the coming and going of the multitude of women in my life.'

'So you would enjoy initiating me?' she retorted sarcastically.

'Maybe I would.' His smile was partly reflective, partly to annoy.

She turned from him. 'I don't know. I just don't know.'

He let her lie there for a few minutes. 'What don't you know?' he said at last, turning her on to her back. He manoeuvred himself until he was leaning over her. 'What's worrying you, my lovely?'

Sweet phrases, she thought, meant for true lovers but meaningless between partners to a marriage of convenience. And she knew better than to think he had any feelings for her except as an outlet for his natural physical desire. How could it be otherwise, when it was only yesterday that they had met?

His fingers trailed her cheek to her chin and down to her throat, sending shivers along her shoulders. 'I'd do nothing to give you pain. I'll never give you cause to regret you married me.'

She said nothing, just gazed into his deep, dark eyes. Her hand lifted and ran over his hair, then moved and playfully tugged at his beard. The whole tempo of his body seemed to change. A light came into his eyes, the heartbeats drummed in his chest as it pressed against her breasts.

Here was the tenderness which she had so sourly told him he did not possess. Under the brutality he had first shown there was, after all, gentleness and consideration. There was no other man she wanted for her husband. She thought fleetingly of Daniel Watling, son of one of her aunt's friends. As soon as her aunt's death had freed her, he had asked her to marry him, but she had refused. He was an uncomplicated, pleasant and entirely unexciting young man. He would have given her a safe marriage, with security and children—if his mother, with whom he lived, had allowed him to!

Her eyes grew aware again and she gazed up at the man leaning over her. This man, who was so different from Daniel, would give her much, much more—wouldn't he? He was waiting, waiting for her answer.

He said softly, 'Where did you go just now, Olivia?'

The way he said her name made her shiver. She looked up at him and smiled. 'No place where you could follow.'

It was as though there was a click in his brain and a door had swung shut on her. 'Do you still doubt my integrity?'

She disregarded the sharpness and played with the collar of his shirt, straightening it so that it did not curl. 'That locked room, Mac?'

His jaw hardened. 'It stays shut.'

Like the many compartments of his mind, she thought, turning her head to one side. Like the many sides of his personality. Like all of his life before they met. All shut, closed to her, even if she became his wife. But who could ever hope to know so much about any man—any woman, for that matter—that there was not even a single secret hidden away?

'I asked you to marry me, Olivia Barnes.' His face softened into a smile. 'Remember?'

She pushed a finger through a buttonhole on his shirt and knew fleetingly that it was a gesture seeking reassurance of his faithfulness, that he would never walk away and leave her.

'I'll marry you, M Delaney,' she whispered, and his mouth came down on ers.

CHAPTER FOUR

ALTHOUGH the mist had largely dispersed, traces remained over the higher hills. A fine rain fell and every time Raff went outside and came back, his fur was damp.

As Olivia rubbed him dry and wiped his muddy paws, Mac looked on, amused. The dog let her do what she liked with him. Now and then he would roll on to his back and she would ruffle his fur and laugh as though fifteen years and more had dropped away.

'You're nothing but a kid at heart,' her fiancé said.

She looked up at him as she knelt beside the dog. 'Not just at heart, Mac.' Their eyes met as the message passed between them.

'Don't be afraid,' was his murmured response, 'that when the time comes I'll forget the fact.'

She coloured and watched as the dog rolled on to his feet. 'I suppose you could say,' she said, half to herself, 'that I missed out on ten years of my youth. I loved my aunt—she looked so much like my mother—but she was very demanding.'

'And you gave your all, as they say, to pander to her every whim?'

As if in excuse, Olivia answered, 'She was a semi-invalid.'

'Maybe,' he said—had she imagined that edge to his voice?—'it was that sympathy and kindness in your nature which I inadvertently played on when I asked you to marry me and which made you accept?'

She frowned, stroking Raff's head. 'Maybe.' Better to let him think it was the truth than to let him know that the first time she had seen him she had experienced the curious sensation of having known him all her life. So loving him had been a mere step away.

They were in the kitchen, having finished their midday meal. Mac had eaten with deliberation, as if determined to regain his strength as quickly as possible.

'I'm going back to bed,' he said, rising. 'Wake me for

the evening meal.'

She nodded, feeling faintly disappointed that during the day he had hardly come near her. But surely, she reproached herself, she did not need a constant display of affection, false as it was, to reassure her that in agreeing to marry such an enigma of a man, she was doing the right thing?

At least, she thought, sighing and washing the dishes, he had offered her marriage and not just half of his bed.

That night she decided to use her sleeping bag in the large family room. Mac had rekindled the fires and she undressed in front of the crackling logs, knowing instinctively that Mac would not come in.

She took a quick bath, shivering in the cold bathroom, pulled on her nightclothes and robe and went down the stairs. At the foot Mac waited. She stood on the bottom step so that she was level with his face.

'You're looking better,' she said breathlessly, but the kiss she had so foolishly expected did not come.

He gave an extremely formal, very accomplished bow. 'My thanks to my own private nurse. Not to mention Mother Nature.' His look became more personal as he looked at her robe. 'I assume you're sharing my bed? You would be welcome.' He smiled mockingly. 'Purely as a sleeping partner, of course. I shall keep my hands——' he corrected himself with a flash of irritation, 'hand to myself.'

She looked away. 'I'll use my sleeping bag tonight, Mac.'

'You don't trust me?' His tone was disconcertingly vicious. 'That locked door?'

Her eyes met his gravely. 'So many locked doors, Mac.'

As she made to pass him, his hand came out. 'No second thoughts?'

'No second thoughts,' she answered, and went on her way.

Next morning Mac entered the kitchen holding a small velvet-covered box. Olivia's heart began to pound.

She looked up at him expectantly and he flicked open the box. It was a wedding ring. 'Mac?' she said, her throat dry.

'This isn't for you,' he answered shortly. 'It was bought to fit another woman's finger. Would you try it for size?'

'You're getting a ring? Today?'

'I'm catching the bus into town. It's one of the three days a week on which it runs.'

He held out the box and Olivia took the ring from its velvet-lined groove. It was a patterned, wide gold band. He handed her the ring and she pushed it on to her wedding finger. 'It's a bit too large,' she told him, easing it off.

He took the ring. 'Do you like the pattern?'

'To be honest, I'd prefer it plain and simple.'

He smiled slightly as if a private thought had amused him. He did not explain. It was another locked door in his mind. 'Plain and simple it will be, partner.' Another swift smile, this time for her, and her heart flipped like a tossed coin.

All the time he was away, the hours dragged. Even Raff, who followed her about, did so dejectedly. Olivia wondered if it was the first time his master had ever left him. She wondered how Mac had acquired the dog and when. She wondered about a lot of things.

. The house was so cold, with the winter air coming in through every broken window pane, it was essential to keep the fires going. She wandered round the outbuildings looking for the coal store. The buildings were in a worse state than the house and she did not like to go farther than a few footsteps into each. The coal was heaped into a corner of a small stone-built shed. Olivia filled a bucket, then returned with another. That, she thought, should keep us going for some hours.

With the dog stretched out beside her in the kitchen, she began to fret, wishing she had asked when the bus came by on its journey back. The transistor radio stood on the kitchen table. Tiring of the endless talking, of which she had not heard a word, she moved the indicator from one station to another, seeking the sound of the kind of music she liked.

The notes of a piano concerto checked her fingers and gripped her mind. She knew the touch of that pianist by heart. He was her idol, and not only hers. He was famed throughout the musical world for his playing—and his devastating good looks.

She was so enraptured by the music that she did not hear the main entrance door open and close. It was not until the kitchen door was opened and Raff made a dive for Mac's feet that Olivia realised her long vigil had ended.

'Mac!' She went towards him, her hands clasped tightly in case they crept around his neck. She saw that his hair had been cut in a fashionable style and that his beard had been trimmed. 'You've been so long I began to worry.'

He did not seem pleased to see her. 'Why?'

Disconcerted by his curtness, she frowned and was glad that she had suppressed any outward show of emotion. 'You haven't been well, for one thing. And,' her eyes moved down, 'your arm. It must make things difficult——'

'To hell with my arm. Turn that thing off!'

'But Mac, I'm listening to it. It's beautiful. Don't you like classical music? If you don't, it's a pity because I love it so much. When my aunt used to settle for the night, I played my records——'

He pushed her aside, examined the radio and found the on-off switch. Then there was silence.

'He's my favourite pianist, Mac. He's playing with the Vienna Philharmonic Orchestra. Why shouldn't I listen? It's my radio!' Her hand went towards it. His came out to grasp hers, throwing it from him.

'He's my one and only pin-up,' she persisted. 'His name's Connal. On my wall at home——' she corrected herself quickly, 'at my aunt's old home, there's a large poster of him—what's the matter,' she tried another smile, 'are you going to be a jealous husband? Don't you like my having a pin-up? But Mac,' as he pushed past her, 'it's only fun. If you had a pin-up girl, I wouldn't mind . . .'

His door closed with a slam.

Olivia dropped into the chair. Raff flopped beside her, and she bent and fondled his ear. 'And I've waited all day for him to come back, Raff,' she whispered, her voice full of tears. Then she shook her head, her heart too full for talking. The man she loved did not share her liking for classical music. In how many other ways did they differ? Why had she agreed to this crazy marriage, anyway?

She had given herself the answer to her question. She loved Mac Delaney and she had to face the fact that, jealous though he might appear of her admiration for another man, he did not love her.

When she called him for the evening meal, she did not hear an answer. He might, she thought, be asleep; he had not yet fully recovered from his illness. When he did emerge from his room, he sank wearily—as much dispirited it seemed, as fatigued—into a chair.

The meal was eaten in silence. Mac seemed preoccupied to the point of being almost unaware of his surroundings. Raff nuzzled up to him, putting up his paw as if he, too, knew that all was not as it should be. Mac patted the paw, then put it from him. When the second paw came up, Mac spoke sharply to Raff who slunk into a corner.

Watching, Olivia thought with a secret smile, If I went to him and put my arm across his shoulder, would he shout at me and send *me* into a corner, too?

As Mac rose, Olivia noticed that he wore the sweater with the worn elbows. 'You've got better sweaters than that, Mac,' she said gently. 'I've seen them. If you'll put another on, I'll mend those sleeves.'

Irritation greeted her offer. 'You're not my wife yet, so there's no need to play the perfect homemaker until my ring is on your finger.'

Her irritation stirred to counter his. 'I'm sorry. I only offered out of——'

'Pity?' he sneered.

She sprang to face him. 'No, you great—great *mountain* of ingratitude! Out of the goodness of my heart, that's what! And because I've been conditioned over the years to mending and more mending. My aunt wasn't exactly poor, but she did like to get her money's worth from everything, including clothes. Since her hands were too crippled by arthritis to sew, *I* did it all. So now you know.'

She busied herself with clearing away, her movements

jerky with suppressed anger. He watched her, foot on a chair, right elbow on the upraised knee. He said casually,

'By the way, we're marrying tomorrow.'

She stopped all action and stared. 'How can we, at such short notice?'

'Civil licence. I bought it while I was in the town. I didn't see any point in delaying the ceremony. It will take place at midday at the register office. I hope you had no hankerings after a more elaborate affair? We haven't got around yet to discussing our personal attitudes to religious beliefs. You don't object to a simple ceremony?'

'No,' Olivia answered quietly, 'I don't object.'

Mac seemed relieved. 'I've booked a car to come for us at eleven o'clock. It's quite a long drive but I've allowed ample time. It may mean a short wait at the other end.' He smiled humourlessly. 'That should give us a little extra time to get to know each other.'

He took a small, square box from his right-hand pocket. 'You can give me this tomorrow. I hope the ring I bought you fits and that you like it. Plain and gold. That's what you said, wasn't it?'

'Of course, but——' she took the box he held out, 'all this must have cost an awful lot of money. The licence, the rings. How——? Where——?'

'Don't worry, I didn't beg or borrow, nor did I steal. I bought them with legal tender. I sold that wedding ring I showed you, and another ring I had in my possession—an engagement ring.'

'Originally intended for—the same woman as the wedding ring?'

'The same woman. So for the moment, my future bedmate, we're well off.'

His choice of the word 'bedmate' made her confused and irritated. He must have intended it as a joke. She couldn't cold-bloodedly . . . The box opened to reveal a signet ring. She frowned, trying in vain to unravel the intermingling initials.

Uncertainly she looked up at him. 'Left hand, Mac? Won't it—hurt?'

'Probably. Let's have a rehearsal, shall we?' There was mockery in his gaze, but the reason for it was beyond her.

With extreme gentleness, she put her fingers round his left wrist, easing his arm upwards. She glanced at him. There was perspiration on his forehead and under his eyes. His breathing was shallow, his jaw gritted.

'Shall I stop?' she asked anxiously. He gave an irritated shake of the head. 'A little more, Mac, just a little more bending . . . Now I'll put the ring on.' She had to work it over the knuckle which itself had grown stiff with disuse. 'There,' she smiled delightedly, 'it's on. You've got long, slim hands, Mac,' she bent and put her cheek to the ring.

He did not move, just stared unseeingly at the floor. She was aware of the pain he must be experiencing, but hoped that the exercise would ease the way to improvement the next time—and the time after that.

'When your physiotherapy-with-kisses session has finished,' he said tightly, 'I'll have my arm back.'

She did not take offence. Slowly she returned the arm to his side and removed the ring. She pushed it back into the box and handed it to him.

'What about witnesses?' she asked.

He turned on his way out. 'We'll find someone. There's bound to be some other wedding guests waiting around.'

'No family, Mac?'

'My mother. She lives in Ireland but is away in Australia at the moment visiting relatives. My father died. He was Irish. You have no one, you said?'

'No one close. Distant cousins and so on. I haven't seen them for years.'

'We seem to be two of a kind.' His smile was twisted. 'A couple of poor, jobless drifters, with no prospects of any better life ahead.'

Olivia frowned. There was so much he did not know about her, almost as much as she did not know about him. She had not told him of the large sum of money her aunt had left her, nor about the substantially-built house near the south coast. But he had barely questioned her about her past, nor her present. He had not seemed interested.

Now he was talking about her future as if her poverty matched his.

Then she remembered the silk shirt and the sweaters, one of them of cashmere, in the wardrobe. Stolen, he had told her, or salvaged from jumble sales. It was surely rare indeed, when stealing or buying from a pile of clothes, to find garments which fitted oneself as exactly, as far as she was able to judge, as those clothes must fit him.

He whistled to Raff who came alive at once. 'Walk,' Mac said, and the dog scampered to the door. Mac turned. 'What will you wear tomorrow? Have you something suitable?'

'I think so. I was on holiday, wasn't I, which meant I had packed one or two special outfits.'

'Just in case,' he mocked, 'you stayed at any three-star hotels.'

If only he knew how near to the truth he was!

'And you, Mac?' she ventured. 'Have you something suitable? Not—not that I'd mind if you wore jeans and jacket . . .'.

'You're a bad liar. You'd mind like hell if I went to our wedding dressed like that.' He returned to the kitchen and took the dog's lead from the hook. 'Don't worry,' he said as he went out, 'I won't let you down.'

Olivia saw Mac only once again that evening. As she came out of the bathroom and made for the stairs, he was half-way up. She waited until he had reached the top and found him beside her. He had unbuttoned his shirt and it hung loose over the old pants he wore.

The hair on his chest, she thought abstractedly, was as dark as the hair on his head. His eyes ensnared hers. She swayed and he put out his hand to support her. Again she experienced the extraordinary feeling of having known this man for an unaccountable length of time. Had she seen him in her dreams, both waking and sleeping?

But she had never, even as a young teenager, woven fantasies about a tall, broad-shouldered, black-haired, bearded man, with eyes which could at times blaze with a passion that arose not from the emotion called love, but something else, some elusive factor beyond most people's imaginings.

'What's wrong?' he queried softly. 'Thinking of running away?'

'Are we——' she swallowed painfully, 'are we doing the right thing, Mac?'

'In getting married?' His eyes dropped and his hand pulled aside her robe. He allowed the toilet bag to fall from under his left arm. Then he lifted that arm slowly, painfully, to rest around her waist, pulling her the length of him. His right hand moved to unfasten the top button of her pyjama jacket. His lips lowered to kiss her throat, moving down to nestle in the hollow between her breasts.

For a long time he stayed thus, breathing in the scent and sweetness of her. When he let her go, she was shivering. 'Mac,' she whispered, her mouth dry, 'Mac . . .'

His right hand cupped her breast. 'Yes,' he said huskily, 'we're doing the right thing.' He bent to retrieve the toilet bag and went on his way.

Olivia had a meagre breakfast. Mac did not have any at all.

He had gone early to the bathroom, while Olivia still lay in her sleeping-bag, emerging from the last dream of the night. As she rolled the bag and put it in a corner, she heard Mac come down and close the door of his room. Olivia took a quick bath and washed her hair, drying it with a towel.

It hung soft and shoulder-length, framing her oval face. There's nothing, she thought, remarkable about me. I've got an ordinary face. Mouth? Nicely curved, she supposed. Eyes? Maybe you could be kind and call them almond-shaped. What was it about her that had made him propose? Not once had he praised her for her looks, her figure or anything about her. Did it matter? she asked herself, gathering her belongings and hurrying down the stairs.

The dress was lavender-coloured and long-sleeved with a deep neckline edged with a paler lavender collar. Around the waist was a long tie belt in the paler shade. The skirt opened to a gentle flare possessing a pleat lined also in the paler colour. Her shoes were in light brown leather, expensive and well-cut. Her handbag and gloves matched the shoes. Round her throat she fastened her aunt's gold necklace.

The door opened and Mac looked her over, leaning sideways against the door. 'My, my,' he murmured. 'Did I say a three-star hotel? Correct that to four-star. Maybe my poor little waif from out of the mist isn't so poor after all.'

'I told you,' she said hurriedly, 'I'd come away for a holiday. I had to have at least one good outfit. This cost a lot of money——'

'I'll bet it did!'

'Why shouldn't I be allowed to have one good——' She stopped. Was she protesting too much? Now she looked him over, and her heart took a tumble over a trip wire. This was a man she hadn't seen before. The suit he wore had not come from his wardrobe.

He seemed to know her thoughts. 'Part of the spoils I've gathered from my life of crime,' he taunted. 'Stowed away in that locked room.'

'But the cut, the cloth, the design. You're lying, Mac. You've only to look at the perfect fit to know that.'

'All right, so I'm lying. Which is a very pleasant accusation to throw at your husband-to-be on our wedding day.'

Husband-to-be? It was then that the situation hit her like a tree crashing on her in a gale. She put shaking hands to her cheeks, feeling them go cold. He had told her frightening tales about himself, laid so many trails which might or might not be false or might lead to bitter truths. And she was on the point of joining her life to his!

'Mac, I——' She hid her face.

'Can't go through with it?' His icy tone lashed her. 'Take me or leave me. Your car has been supplied with sufficient petrol to get you to the nearest filling station. Did I forget to tell you? I called in at a garage in the town yesterday and paid a mechanic to bring out a large can of fuel. He had to pass this way as he went home. So you're free, Olivia, to pack your belongings and go. Out of my life, unscathed, unviolated and unburdened by a husband who's only half a man.'

His eyes were as brittle as his voice as they watched her unwaveringly. She could not speak, could scarcely even think. Did she really mean so little to this man that he could let her run away—and on the day of their intended marriage—never to see her again?

There were a few steps between them, but they might as well have been on different planets. Wearily he turned to go, pulling at his tie as if to free himself of its suffocating tightness.

'No, no! I'm staying, Mac, I'm staying. Don't, don't!' She put herself in front of him and reached up, tightening the knot again.

There was the crunch of wheels outside. Olivia picked up the warm camel coat she had brought with her from home. It swung from her shoulders, protecting her from the chill March air. Raff came swerving into the room.

'Back, boy,' Mac ordered, going into the inner lobby. 'Come on. We'll see you later. There's food and water to keep you going and the back door's open if you need to go out.' He roughed up the dog's fur. As the door closed, Raff sat on his haunches and barked his indignation.

On his way to the car, Mac pulled on a sheepskin jacket. Olivia tried to hide her astonishment. Yet another expensive item of clothing she had never seen before. Had that also come from the locked room?

The reception area at the register office was busy. A man who seemed to be friend to everyone, regardless of which wedding party he attached himself to, came over to Olivia and Mac.

'You a happy couple, too?' he asked. Mac nodded briefly. The young man looked around. 'No relatives, no guests?'

Olivia smiled tautly. 'No hangers-on, no.'

The man laughed. He eyed them curiously. 'Come from these parts?'

'Well——' Olivia began, but Mac broke in, 'Yes and no.'

The young man laughed again. 'Now that's what I call evading the question.'

'Mac,' Olivia said quietly, 'what about witnesses?'

Mac sighed irritably, then looked at the man. 'I didn't catch your name?'

'Ivens, Pete Ivens. I'm here to attend the wedding of a local Farmers' Club beauty queen. You need a witness? Can I be of service? I could get another witness for you.' He indicated some elaborately dressed people across the room. 'They're waiting for the beauty queen, too. Relatives of hers.'

'That's very kind of you,' Olivia said quickly, anticipating Mac's curt refusal.

'Glad to be of service on such a special day,' said the young man, and left them.

Mac looked uneasily after him and Olivia wondered why. He did not explain. The man called Ivens returned, telling them that an aunt of the beauty queen would be delighted to act as the second witness to their wedding. It seemed that the young woman for whom they were all waiting was due to be married half an hour after midday.

Olivia slipped off her coat and helped Mac with his. Peter Ivens watched closely as she eased the sleeve from Mac's left arm. He looked puzzled but did not comment.

'Don't take your coats in,' he advised. 'Someone here will look after them. Everyone's happy and willing to oblige when they come to a wedding.'

Somebody did take the coats and exactly on time, Olivia preceded Mac into the large room in which the marriage ceremony was to take place. It was filled with flowers, their colours and scents delighting already heightened emotions. The lady who had agreed to act as the second witness came forward and followed, Peter Ivens entering last and closing the door.

The ceremony was solemn but brief. It was Mac who spoke first, repeating the words after the registrar had spoken them. In a daze, and only half aware of where she was, or why she was there at all, Olivia heard Mac say,

'I, Macaire Connal Delaney, do take thee, Olivia Sarah Barnes, to be my lawful wedded wife . . .'

Olivia swayed, her muddled brain trying crazily to work out the bewildering problem which had been thrust before it.

She heard herself repeat, after the registrar, 'I, Olivia Sarah Barnes, do take thee, Macaire Connal Delaney, to be my lawful wedded husband ...' When at last she had finished speaking, she gazed up at him, trying to mouth his name. No sound came. *Macaire Connal Delaney, Macaire Connal* ...

He was reaching for her hand, pushing on to it the wedding ring, holding out to her the ring to be placed on his finger. His left arm was a blur as she lifted it, with infinite gentleness, until it was possible for her to slip the signet ring on to his marriage finger. It registered somewhere in her mind that his arm had bent just a little more easily than before.

At the registrar's request, they signed their names. The two witnesses followed with theirs. They shook the newly-married couple's hands and discreetly disappeared. The registrar gently and sincerely wished them every possible happiness and Mac thanked him with apparently equally sincere gratitude.

Olivia wondered if her legs would carry her to the door. It seemed such a long way ... Mac's arm went round her waist. He appeared to sense her bewilderment and seemed to realise that, both physically and mentally, she had received a deep shock.

Peter Ivens came up to them, handing them their coats. 'I suppose there's no reception for you two? Just a quiet wedding?' Mac nodded, his eyes guarded, but Peter Ivens' face showed nothing but good nature and a desire to please. 'No photographer, either?' He did not wait for an answer. 'Look, there's a special wedding photographer out there, says he's waiting for the beauty queen. You're early, she's late, so he's got a bit of time to spare. Says he's willing to take four or five for you, usual rates, nothing outrageous. What about it?'

'Olivia?' She looked up. Her eyes did not seem to be focusing properly.

'It would be nice, Mac,' she whispered, 'to have some kind of record, a picture or two ...' *Just to show me, in later years, when our ways have parted, as part they must* because of what I now know about you, that it wasn't all a dream, that once I was your wife . . .

'Fair enough. Mr Ivens, my wife is willing, and because she wishes it, so am I.'

His wife, Olivia thought, Macaire Connal's wife! The pianist who, she had told Mac, was her favourite, a picture of whom she had put on her wall at home . . . They posed at the top of the steps, with the rounded archway of the register office door acting as a frame. They smiled—at least Olivia knew that she smiled. Whether Mac had managed to do so, she would not know until she saw the photographs.

While Peter Ivens took their coats again, the photographer gave instructions. 'Look into each other's eyes. Put your arm round her waist, sir. Not your left arm? Change places then, and make it your right arm. That's it. Smile now—fine.'

'When———?' Olivia asked.

'Just give me your name and address,' the photographer said, producing a notebook, 'and I'll send them. No obligation to buy.'

'The name is Delaney. We'll collect,' Mac said sharply.

'No need, sir———'

'Send them to the post office,' Mac named the village near which they lived. 'I'll inform the postmaster that they're coming, and he'll hold them for me.'

He turned to Peter Ivens, who still lingered. Mac took their coats, slipping Olivia's round her shoulders and carrying his own. 'Thank you for your help, Mr Ivens. My wife and I have appreciated it. Goodbye.' Mac took Olivia's arm and began to propel her away.

But Peter Ivens was proving more difficult to remove than it seemed Mac had anticipated. 'Sudden, this marriage, sir?' the man asked, following them. 'Was it love at first sight, sir?' No response. 'Mrs Delaney?' It took a few seconds for the name to register.

'Er—yes—yes, it was, wasn't it, Mac? We fell in love———'

'The moment you set eyes on each other, eh? And when

was that, Mrs Delaney? Just a rough estimate?'

'Look, Mr Ivens,' Mac intervened, 'we're newlyweds. We'd like some time alone. We want to gaze into each other's eyes.' His smile was strained. 'You do understand? So will you please exercise the discretion I know you possess and allow us to enjoy this rather special day?'

Olivia wondered at the underlying criticism in Mac's words, at the edge to his voice.

Peter Ivens' eyes grew wary, but his reply was pleasant enough. 'Of course I understand, Mr Delaney. I'm the soul of discretion. And anyway, here comes the bride I've been waiting for. Every happiness, you two.' He lifted his hand and walked away.

In the car which had been waiting for them, Mac said, 'Don't talk, just don't say a word. Driver, take us to the Planets Hotel.'

'But, Mac——'

'I've reserved a table for two.'

'But it's so expensive there, Mac. I looked it up on my way north, when I was planning where to stay, but it was beyond my means.'

'It's not beyond mine, Olivia. There's no need for me to pretend any more. As you must have guessed by now, I'm a rich man.' There was a kind of suppressed savagery in his voice. He looked down at his injured arm. 'It's all I've got left—my recordings and the money they bring.'

'Mac,' Olivia whispered hoarsely, 'you've got me.'

He looked at her, his dark eyes unreadable. He said nothing. They had arrived at the hotel. 'We'll send in the bill, sir,' the driver said.

Mac reached into his inner pocket. 'I'd rather pay now.'

'As you wish, sir. I'll have to contact them by this.' He indicated the radio-telephone in the cab. 'Find out how much.'

'We'll be waiting in the entrance lobby,' said Mac, as the driver helped them from the car. Mac walked by Olivia's side into the hotel. 'Go to the cloakroom,' he told her. 'Leave your coat there.'

By the time she had returned, Mac was seated on a sofa and holding the large menu. There were two drinks on a table beside him. The cab driver was making for the swing doors, a satisfied smile on his face. There was no doubt that his tip had been a large one.

As soon as Olivia appeared a waiter approached and gave her a menu. The choice was so great she was confused. 'You choose, Mac,' she said, smiling. 'I'm not used to such exotic surroundings.'

'Poor little poor girl, eh?' He smiled suddenly and Olivia's heart began to dance. 'No matter. My career came to an end a little over a year ago. One day our money will run out, then you can revert to the simple, struggling life you're accustomed to.'

The waiter returned and Mac gave their order. When he was offered the wine list, he went straight to the champagnes, chose, and asked to be shown to their table. They were led over dark red carpet to an alcove which contained a table with two place settings.

Olivia gazed across the table at the man she had married less than one hour before. He was a stranger again, but of another kind. He was not the poor, injured man defying convention and the ill-fortune which had turned him into a near-hermit. Nor was he the person who had met her so belligerently at the door of his crumbling, time-battered farmhouse.

This man possessed a cynical knowledge of the world and its ways, a self-confidence bordering on the imperious, an ability to take charge, give orders and receive in return nothing less than his exact requirements.

He frightened her now as he had frightened her before, but in a very different way. The so-called 'crimes' he had claimed he had committed were as nothing when compared with the hidden fires and passions she sensed dwelt beneath the decisive, authoritative manner he had displayed since they had seen each other earlier that morning.

His public life prior to his accident she knew by heart, but his private way of life before he adopted his present manner of living was as complete a mystery to her as the contents of that locked room at the farmhouse. But she could hazard a guess, and the vision she conjured up of his former life-style made her go cold.

During lunch they talked little, but when they did speak it was of general matters. It was as though Mac did not wish her to question him on any subject approaching the personal. Only once, when they drank the champagne, did his thoughts seem to return from a distant place and acknowledge that this was a special occasion.

'To our future together, my girl out of the mist.' They touched glasses and drank, smiling at each other over the rims. His smile made her reach out her hand and it was captured at once by his. He looked at the wedding ring he had so recently put there and said,

'That looks lonely. I have something to give you.' He felt in his right-hand pocket and pulled out a box. With his thumb he eased open the lid to reveal a solitaire diamond set in white and yellow gold. 'I hope its design is "simple" enough for your tastes.' His quick smile was crooked. He took her left hand again and pushed the diamond ring into place.

Olivia shook her head, breathless and laughing. 'First we get married, then we get engaged! How crazy can you get, Mac?'

He looked at her through narrowed eyes. 'I can do a lot better than this, my lovely. Our married life hasn't even started yet.'

Colour warmed her cheeks and she said, 'Really, darling, you needn't have bothered.'

He caught her wrist and said with mock-menace, 'So you refuse to become engaged to me?'

Laughter bubbled over and she answered, 'If you insist, kind sir.' His thumb moved caressingly over the inner part of her wrist. Her eyes sought his and wandered over his face and beard. 'Do you know, Mac, when I first saw you, I had an odd feeling that I knew you, that I'd met you somewhere. Strange, now that I know, how I couldn't place you.'

He released her wrist and she went on, 'The times I've

gazed at that giant-sized poster of you on my bedroom wall! When I saw you, I think it was the beard that fooled me. Plus, of course, the ragged jeans, the long hair, not to mention the illness that made you so pale and weak. And bad-tempered.'

He laughed shortly. 'If you think that was bad, wait until you've been married to me for a few more weeks! You'll wonder what's knocked you flying. Metaphorically, of course.' His eyes grew warm and he reached out for her hand again, turning the palm as if trying to read the future there. 'Will you be my left hand, my lovely?'

Her heart was in her eyes as she nodded. A few moments later, she shook her head. He frowned.

'Your left hand will regain its use, darling,' she insisted. 'I know it will, I just know!'

He released her hand and withdrew into himself.

'Mac,' she pleaded, 'you can't go on for ever depriving people of the pleasure of listening to your wonderful performances.'

'You regard my playing of the piano in public as a "duty"?'

'Of course not. You're deliberately misunderstanding my meaning.'

'I don't think so. You're telling me I'm under an obligation to put myself through hell in trying to regain my concert form, not because of my wish to express the music I carry inside me, but simply to please others. I'm sorry to disappoint you,' Olivia was dismayed by his chilling tone, 'but my days of piano playing are over.'

There the subject ended. She could not plead with him within the hearing of the hotel's many patrons. Instead she tried, successfully, to change the direction of the conversation.

'It seems strange now,' she reflected with a smile, 'to think about those terrible things you said about yourself when I arrived on your doorstep the other day, the threats you made——'

'Why didn't they drive you away?'

She frowned. 'I don't really understand that myself. It

must have been that "odd" feeling I had about you. Remember how you said, "How the culture clings"?' He pushed around his empty coffee cup but did not answer. 'Mac, am I really your wife?'

His left hand came slowly out of his pocket. Olivia wondered if it was her imagination or whether it was moving just a little more easily. He shot back his cuff to consult a gold watch she had never seen before.

'Nearly three hours ago,' he said, 'we went through a ceremony.' He indicated his own ring, then hers. 'Which proves you're my wife.' He smiled and there was a gleam in his eyes. 'At present, in name only, but not for long. Madam, I have it in mind to make room for you tonight in my bed. So, take warning before the day's over——'

'Mac, people will hear!'

'What does it matter? You're mine and no one, nothing, can take you away.'

'No one,' she echoed, 'nothing, will take me away.'

Across the restaurant a shout of laughter rose from a crowd of people. Involuntarily, Olivia shivered. The sound had seemed to mock the solemnity of the promise she had just made.

It was, for Olivia, a strange homecoming. 'I've lived here for less than a week,' she commented, dropping her coat on to a chair, 'yet I look on it already as home.'

Mac, crouched down and playing roughly with Raff who had bounded to greet them, looked up at her. He smiled faintly. 'I've lost count of how many times you've walked away from it. Yet each time you came back. Why?'

Raff growled in play.

Olivia smiled impishly. 'There must be something about the place. You, for instance.'

Mac rose, using his right hand to brush himself free of dog's hairs. 'I don't kid myself. Nor do I believe you love me, not after five or so days.'

It was like a fist in her face. It sent her, mentally, staggering. 'Then why did I marry you?' she asked, bewildered.

He went to her, forcing up her chin. 'Suppose you tell me.'

'I thought you knew. I love you.'

'You're a good liar, my precious.' He dropped his hold on her chin. 'I could—almost—bring myself to believe you, provided I tried hard enough.'

Here was the man she had first known, the man who had reluctantly allowed her into his living-place for just one night. He hadn't disappeared, that man with revenge in his heart, who had tried to shut out the world because of the lost love of a woman.

Mac went from the room and Olivia bent to stroke the dog, taking the paw he solemnly offered. To Raff, she thought, while they had been away there had simply been the loneliness and endless waiting. To him, the two people for whom he had waited had returned to the house exactly as they had left it. He could not know that for one of them at least there had been a cataclysmic alteration in her whole way of life.

Her car was parked outside. Mac had asked the driver they had hired for the return journey to drop them near the small blue car. They had transferred into it and Olivia had driven it down the track and into the muddy farmyard. There was more than enough petrol in the tank, Mac had told her, to take her a good many miles.

Braking outside the tumbledown building, Olivia had smiled. 'Is that a hint?'

'Just try to get away from me now,' Mac had answered. 'Just try.'

There had been no humour in his tone, no tenderness, only a cold, harsh sound which she was certain was there as a result of past events. The girl he had once loved had 'got away', leaving him with only the two expensive rings and the smouldering embers of the love he had felt for her.

'I'll put those embers out,' Olivia had vowed. 'I'll stamp on them until not even the ashes of that love are left.' And with that satisfying thought, she had followed him into the house.

CHAPTER FIVE

OLIVIA cooked the evening meal. Mac offered to help, but at first she would not let him.

'I insist,' he told her. 'I might be a bit slow, but since there's no great hurry, it doesn't matter.'

'But your arm——'

'I want to exercise it.'

Hope leapt into her eyes. 'Why, Mac?'

'All the better to make love to you, my dear,' he said, imitating the voice of the disguised wolf in Red Riding Hood.

She laughed, bending to kiss the ring she had placed on his finger. He was as slow in working as he had warned. He was no faster drying the dishes, either, but in her heart, Olivia was delighted to see him making the attempt, even though it was plain that every movement gave him pain. If she could be the incentive to his return to the world of music, then she would do all in her power to urge him on.

Afterwards, they shared the threadbare armchair in the room Olivia had used for sleeping. The fire burned in the grate, and as the evening grew darker, shadows danced across the ceiling and all around the walls. Olivia rested her head against Mac's chest, while her arms held him loosely round the waist.

His right arm pulled her closely against him, and as his left arm came slowly, slowly towards her, she held her breath, only to release it in an upsurge of delight as his left hand cupped her breast. For some time they sat, Mac deep in his thoughts which, as the firelight played over his strong features, seemed as though they were entirely pleasing.

Olivia, filled with a rising, anticipatory joy, had long ago suspended all thought, immersing herself instead in the touch of him, his masculine scent, the sound of his strong heartbeat beneath her ear.

'Mac,' she said at last, 'wouldn't treatment help to restore the strength to your arm?'

He smiled. 'Treatment would take quite a long time, and I'm not willing to wait that long before I make love to you!'

'That's not what I mean, Mac. I mean——' she looked, frowning, into his face, 'your music, your career.'

His body stiffened. 'No treatment, thanks.' His abrupt dismissal of her suggestion puzzled her.

'I can't understand your attitude,' she argued. 'Other people with an injury like yours would have moved heaven and earth——'

'I'm not "other people". Nor do I believe in heaven. Hell maybe, but——'

'Do you know what I think?'

'I don't particularly want to know, as the whole subject grates, but you're determined to tell me.'

'Yes, I am.' She sat up, deaf to the warnings whispering from the corners of her mind. 'I think you've done nothing about it because you want pity——'

The flames of the fire seemed to have transferred themselves to his eyes. He grasped a handful of her hair, pulling back her head. 'Is that why you married me? You were sorry for me, hated to see a fellow human being, especially one with a bit of youth and vitality left in him, mouldering away in self-imposed exile——'

She tried to shake her head, but his hold on her hair was too firm. 'Oh, Mac, you've got it all wrong.' Now she was counting the cost of having ignored those warnings. She had trodden with heavy feet where angels would have been scared to go on tiptoe. The evening's tranquillity had gone beyond recall.

He released her hair, pushed her from his lap and stood up. His hands found his pockets, the right hand easily, the left painfully. 'You said you had a feeling of having known me before. Therefore I believe that subconsciously you did recognise me. The reason you married me was through hero-worship, not love,' she was shaking her head violently, 'with the intention eventually of turning me back into that "idol" you carry in your mind.'

'Mac, Mac,' tears were blurring her vision, 'you're so wrong . . .'

He disregarded her words. 'Even now you don't see me as a real man. To you, I'm still a famous pianist. This past week you've been flattered by my attentions—not as a man, but because of all that I represent. Now, having "caught" me, you're going to start your campaign. You're going to do everything in your power to get me to return to being that musician-superstar who was fortunate enough to be born with looks that dazzled and whom women, yourself included, worshipped from afar.'

'How can you say such things,' she whispered, 'only a few hours after I joined my life to yours?' She was appalled that on their wedding day they had quarrelled with such bitterness. She was distressed by his lack of trust in her—frightened, too, because there was some truth in his assertions. Hadn't she, only half an hour ago, told herself that she would do everything in her power to get him to return to his music?

'But it would be for your sake,' she defended herself, 'not mine. Not anyone else's but your own. You were a brilliant pianist, Mac, and you will be again.'

'Do you realise,' he said, holding his temper on a tight rein, 'exactly what it would mean if I were to start on that long climb back to the top? It would mean a period of physiotherapy on my arm, months of practice, of complete dedication, totally shutting out the world—including you,' he added with a gleam of cruelty. 'Would you,' he asked maliciously, 'be able to live without me for so long, without the fulfilment I shall give you, and which in time you'll come to expect as your right?'

Her eyes were large and full of appeal as they sought his. 'I'd sacrifice anything, Mac, if it meant your returning to——'

He swung away and strode out and she heard a muttered curse as the dog tried to follow him into the bedroom. The door slammed. Raff whimpered, then joined Olivia, who sank back into the armchair. The fire was dying down, the room growing cool. Already she was missing the warm, enveloping arms of her husband.

As the time passed, Olivia grew increasingly weary of waiting for Mac to return to her. She took her robe which had been folded and placed on top of the rolled-up sleeping bag, and went upstairs.

The bath refreshed her and while she was rubbing herself dry she heard Mac calling the dog into the house. A door closed, then another. It seemed that Mac had shut himself into his room again. Despondent now, Olivia went down the stairs and curled up in the armchair, staring at the dying fire. How much longer was he going to pretend she did not exist?

When he finally went upstairs, she crept into his room, hoping to find there some clue as to his intentions. It took only moments to find it. Spread out over the bed was the sheerest flame-coloured nightgown she had ever seen. It was ankle-length and draped from the shoulders to a plunging neckline and a tie belt. He could not have told her more clearly that their wedding night was to be no sham.

With loving hands she lifted the garment and held it against her cheek. He could not have given her a more beautiful wedding gift. Moments later it was over her head and cascading in an exciting swirl to touch her feet. She pulled on her robe and returned to the other room to collect her personal belongings, taking them into Mac's—and now her—room.

He had, she discovered, even emptied a drawer for her clothes. She put her cosmetics on the small dressing-table and ran a comb through her hair. She opened her robe just before removing it and looked down at herself. Immediately her impulse was to cover herself again. Idiot, she thought, I'm twenty-six, I'm old enough to know better. I'm a bride and this is the first night of my marriage—*and I'm as nervous and scared as a*——

'Olivia.' His voice came from the doorway and she turned. He was stripped to the waist. Freed now from the

weight of neglected illness, his shoulders were broadened
to reveal a toughness which, as she had tended him at the
height of his fever, she had only been able to guess at.

His body was lean, his arms strong with a strength which
had no doubt been developed during the course of his brilliant musical career. His height was commanding now that
his health had returned. The restrained power within his relaxed body had her senses stirring, her eyes bright with
admiration and also with wonder that this handsome
stranger was her husband.

His eyes were mocking and hooded as he watched her
watching him. His lips curved in a smile full of a knowledge
of which she was ignorant. His chin bore a dent of determination and obduracy. *His chin!*

'Mac,' she whispered, 'you've shaved off your beard!'

'Clever girl,' was his sardonic comment. 'Go to the top
of the class.'

'Mac—why?'

'I'll tell you why, my lovely. To fulfil your feminine
fantasies, to give you the consummate pleasure of being
made love to by the man—the flesh and blood version—
who apparently adorns the wall of your bedroom in your
own home. Seduced not in your dreams, honey, but for
real.'

His sarcasm grazed her sensibilities. This was not how
she had imagined their first night together. But had she
foolishly imagined a running into each other's arms, a
mutual delight in becoming as one at last? She was the
wife of a disappointed man—it was necessary to repeat that
to herself many times, so that it would be absorbed into her
very system—not an eager youth in love for the first time.
This man was not in love with her, never would be.

'Why are you angry with me, Mac? Do you still hold it
against me for telling you how much I long to hear you play
again?'

He did not reply. His left arm lifted slowly. 'Come to me,
my lovely.'

'My lovely,' he kept saying, a beautiful endearment,
although coming from him, quite meaningless, but he was

making it easier for her. He straightened and walked a pace or two into the room, leaving her to close the gap between them.

He opened her robe, drew it from her shoulders and dropped it to the floor. His eyes wandered over her, bright with possessiveness, absorbing, as if she were a painting, every detail of the shapeliness and enticements beneath the transparent gown.

'You're beautiful,' he murmured, his hand lifting to rest against her throat, his thumb stroking beneath her ear and feeling for the throbbing pulse in her neck. He tipped up her face a little. 'Did you like my present?'

'It's wonderful,' she whispered.

'Good, because now you're going to give me a present, sweetheart—yourself.'

His right arm encircled her waist, pulling her against the hard masculinity of his body. His lips descended, parting hers and taking his fill of the sweetness her mouth contained. Never in her life had she been kissed in so intimate a fashion. As the kiss went on, her shyness receded and her arms locked round his neck.

She felt herself being propelled towards the bed, eased down and still the kiss went on. He was beside her, caressing her into complete submission. When he slipped the gown from her shoulders and his lips released hers, only to seek the fullness of her breasts, her barriers were gone.

She wanted only to give and to receive, to abandon herself totally to every one of his demands, to the feel of him urgently, ardently above her, his hips, his thighs against her, penetrating to the very essence of her being. She was drunk with love, with desire and with passion—her own and his. Through a haze she heard him whisper, 'It's been so long, my love, so long . . .'

Then, with a gentleness of which she had not thought him capable, he possessed her utterly and her joy was complete.

Next morning it was Sunday, but in the heart of the Yorkshire moors, the silence was no deeper than it usually was, the birds sang no more rapturously than was their habit.

It was, Olivia decided, awakening from the deepest sleep she had ever slept, just that the contentment of her body and mind and the happiness that pulsated through her veins made the countryside seem more peaceful and gave the birdsong a greater purity.

Mac's arms were round her, holding her the length of him. His eyes were closed. The tips of her fingers rubbed the hair on his chest, lifted to outline the unfamiliar shape of his chin, pressing playfully against the cleft. Her forefinger ran around the sensual curve of his lips. They opened swiftly and his teeth fastened on her finger. She squealed and he let it go, laughing down at her.

She remembered how, in the darkness of the night, he had reached out for her and their desire had rekindled. The rapture of the intermingling of their bodies for the second time had been, if possible, even greater than before.

She sighed and curled into him, resting her cheek against his chest. 'Mac, oh, Mac, I love you.' He stroked her hair, using, she noticed, his left hand. It felt as if he were concentrating on every movement his arm made, willing it to continue, despite the pain it was giving him. At last the stroking stopped and she closed her eyes. 'Do you love me, Mac?'

Her body tensed against his. Why was the answer so long in coming? He said at last, '*Never seek to tell thy love, Love that never told can be . . .*'

She waited for him to continue, but he said no more. She took him up. '*I told my love, I told my love, I told him all my heart . . . Ah! he did depart!*' She looked up at him. 'I've changed the sex, but I don't think William Blake would have minded.'

'I'll finish it as he wrote it. *Soon after she was gone from me. A traveller came by, Silently, invisibly, He took her with a sigh.*' He pulled her closer, running his hand caressingly over her body. 'So you see, my lovely, why I gave you no answer.'

'But Mac, I'll never leave you, never!'

In reply, his mouth sought hers hungrily, almost angrily, and they were lost to the world.

The day melted away. It was as if they could not bear to be parted for more than a few minutes. When Mac took Raff for a walk, Olivia joined them, holding Mac's hand and with her other, the dog's leash whenever they met a road.

The name tag, Olivia noticed, had been replaced on Raff's collar. When she bent down to read the words engraved on the rectangle of hallmarked gold, she was not surprised that his owner, wishing to keep his own identity a secret, had removed it on her arrival.

Raff, it said on one side. On the other—owner, Macaire Connal Delancy. Please return this animal to the police station . . . There followed the name of a town in the county of Surrey. Mac waited patiently until she had ended her inspection, then said, a little edgily, 'Come on.'

She put her fingers lightly in those of his left hand and asked, 'Is that where your real home is?' She named the town.

'It's in Surrey, yes, but some distance from that town.'

After their evening meal, they shared a fireside chair in the kitchen. Olivia lay against Mac. His arms were around her and she thought and dreamed and thought again . . . about Mac's life before he came there, about the woman he had 'lost', about the times she had been to the concerts he had given, or watched him on television. It was then that her marriage to him seemed like something in a dream, unarguably real while sleep was in charge of the mind, but when consciousness crept back, reality became elusive and shadowy and even turned into pure fantasy.

'How is it,' Mac said, breaking the silence, 'that no other man has discovered you before?'

So he had been thinking about her, maybe wondering about her life before they met as she had been wondering about his. 'Well,' she pulled at the polo collar of his sweater, tugging it straight, 'there is—was—a man, the son of a friend of my aunt's. He lives—lived—just round the corner. He's in his mid-twenties.'

'Now we're hearing about the secret life of Olivia Barnes, are we?' her husband said teasingly.

'Delaney,' she said, 'Olivia Delaney.' She planted a kiss on his chin. 'Not really, no. It was all very innocent. When my aunt could spare me, he took me out. Once he asked me to marry him.'

'Plainly you didn't. But why not?'

'I didn't love him,' she said simply. She met Mac's eyes unflinchingly as they gave her a quizzical look.

'So you were determined to marry for love?'

'Of course.'

'But you married me, hardly knowing me.'

'Yes.'

He laughed, his eyes bright. 'End of discussion?'

A pause, then, 'Yes.'

He laughed again. She lifted his hand and studied the long fingers and wondered that they could once have produced such sounds that the listeners' hearts, their very beings, felt indescribably uplifted. For a few moments he allowed her to play with his hand. Then he said, 'Don't say it.'

'That I want to hear you play again? No, no, of course not.'

His head lifted from the chair back. 'You have said it, haven't you?'

She flinched at his change of tone. 'Only because—oh, yes, I suppose I have. Mac,' she persisted in spite of the caution which was urging her to stop, 'where does the music you produce come from? Not just from your fingers, but——'

'From my brain, my body, my emotions, my experience of life. Not to mention,' he added dryly, 'the technique I've learnt and absorbed into my playing. Now will you be quiet?'

'But Mac——'

He stirred. 'There's only one way for a man to silence his woman,' he pushed her from his lap and stood up. 'One day I shall carry you—that's a promise. Until then ...'

With his right arm about her waist, he urged her towards the bedroom.

Olivia smiled up at him radiantly. She did not resist.

Next morning being Monday, Olivia decided it was time to clean their living area.

Mac announced that the electricity generator needed attention and that if she wanted his help she would find him there. Raff divided his time between the two of them, sometimes racing indoors and walking on the scrubbed floors. Olivia scolded him affectionately and wiped away his pawmarks.

She made her way to the bathroom, cleaning it thoroughly. As she returned to the top of the stairs, she passed the locked room. Lowering the pail of water to the floor, she stared at the key. It had never been in place in the lock before, so why was it there now? To test her trustworthiness? To tempt her? Or to tell her that, now she was Mac's wife, he had no secrets from her?

Deciding after long deliberation that the third possibility must be the correct one, she moved her hand towards the key—then drew back. She had remembered the blood-chilling claims Mac had made about its contents. However, now that she knew the truth about him, the room could surely hold no terrors for her, and she dismissed her fears.

At first sight the contents made little impression. The room appeared once to have been an office. There was a large, slightly battered roll-top desk. The lid was raised revealing shallow drawers and slots. There was an ancient swivel chair whose leather-covered seat was torn in places. The windows were uncovered, giving a view across the moorland which was magnificent in the morning sunshine.

There was a wide fireplace above which was a ceiling-high mirror. Olivia's glance roved and she saw in one of the wide alcoves a display of modern hi-fi equipment. It must have been bought, she calculated, at considerable cost. Nearby there were racks of records. One or two had been extracted and left on a table. On one of the record sleeves was a portrait of Macaire Connal in the act of playing the piano.

Olivia picked up the record sleeve and studied the en-larged photograph wistfully, her eyes lingering with some-thing near to veneration on the handsome profile. With deep compassion she looked at that left hand. Once he had had complete control over its movements, but she had seen it resting uselessly at his side or being lifted and used with undoubted pain. The hand, ringless in the photograph, now carried the signet ring which she had placed on his finger on their wedding day.

Putting down the record, she moved to the desk. She had intended to dust it, but something caught her eye. Pushed into one of the slots was a collection of press cut-tings. Anxious to read anything which was even remotely connected with her husband's past achievements, she pulled them out and separated them so that they lay flat on the desk.

It was not long before she realised that the cuttings had little to do with Macaire Connal's skill as a concert pianist. There were photographs of Macaire, but he was not alone. Hanging on to his arm and gazing adoringly up at him was a woman also known to Olivia, and who herself was a famous figure in the musical world.

The paragraph ran, 'The beautiful and celebrated opera star, Annetta Brambella, stakes her claim to Macaire Con-nal, the man soon to become her husband. He, like his wife-to-be, is famed throughout the world for his musical skill—as a concert pianist of superb talent and sensitivity. The handsome couple should make a fine team, both as life partners and musical collaborators.

'Miss Brambella and Mr Connal have known each other for some time. "We are very excellent friends," Miss Brambella told me in her very excellent English. The news of their coming marriage was leaked to the press by an unknown source. Mr Connal expressed irritation at the leak, but his fiancée did not seem to be too upset . . .'

Unclenching her hand and dropping the yellow duster, Olivia studied the picture of Macaire's ex-fiancée. Annetta Brambella was black-haired—like himself—with dark, pas-

sionate eyes and a figure which would never pass unnoticed in a crowd.

Another cutting caught Olivia's eyes. The heading ran,
'Famous pianist hurt in car accident.' In smaller print,
'Crashed his car after fiancée left him to go to another man.'
The reporter filled in the details. 'Macaire Connal, world-
renowned virtuoso of the piano, skidded into a brick wall
and was badly injured yesterday.'

The newspaper cutting was about eighteen months old.
The report continued, 'Mr Connal's legs were broken, his
ribs fractured and his left arm badly damaged. *He'll play
again*, his manager said, but Macaire Connal himself was
less optimistic. "Never again," he asserted.

'It may never be known what caused the crash,' the report went on. 'Mr Connal refused to comment, but those
closest to him said he was so deeply hurt by his fiancée's
desertion only three days before their wedding, he might
never get over it. Questioned further, Mr Connal said he
would say only one more thing—that he would never trust
a woman again.

'His embittered attitude,' the writer elaborated, 'might
give those to whom his performances have meant so much
a clue as to why his car, without any apparent reason, suddenly went out of control, causing an accident which inflicted on him extensive injuries. Let Macaire Connal have
the last word. *I'll never marry*, he declared. Well,' the report
finished, 'we shall see. My only comment is that it would
take a clever woman indeed to storm Macaire Connal's
barriers again!'

Olivia leaned back in the chair. She remembered what
Mac had said when she had entered the farmhouse for the
second time, after he had sent her away.

Warm me, he'd said, *let your warmth bring me back to
life. I've lost so many things—a woman, a whole world* . . .

She remembered, too, the way he had pulled her close
until they had touched. She could not check the tears which
sprang—of sympathy and understanding . . .

'I thought I'd find you here.'

Olivia rubbed her palms over her eyes and swung round. The swivel chair creaked. 'The key was in the lock,' she said defensively.

'So it was. And, being a woman, you couldn't resist its invitation. You had to turn it and, in doing so, unlocked Pandora's Box.' He strolled in. 'Now you know so much more about me than you did before becoming my wife, does it make you any happier?'

She regarded him with dismay. The man she had married had gone. The cool-eyed, cold-hearted stranger had returned. All that was missing was the beard, the long hair and the ragged clothes. He tugged his sweater over his head and threw it on an upright chair. His hair was in disarray from the sweater passing over it and she wanted to run to him and smooth it down.

His jeans were tight as though he had increased just a little in weight since last wearing them. The brown belt around the waist rested on lean hips, his shirt was partly unbuttoned, showing the dark hair she had rubbed dry during his fever.

'No,' she answered at last, 'it makes me no happier to know how much you loved the woman who let you down, or how you went to pieces when she left you for another man.'

'I did not go to pieces.' His tone was curt, his eyes like ice.

'You crashed the car after she left you.'

'Correction, if you please. After a perfomance.'

'So you gave a performance after she left you. It makes no difference. You probably drank too much to drown your sorrows and——'

In two strides he was facing her and—miraculously—both his hands came up. They seized her arms and shook her unmercifully. 'You'll retract that statement, my girl!' He was white with anger and she stammered an apology. He dropped his left arm and she knew that he was pale with pain, also, by the way his right hand went protectively to hold his left arm.

'All right,' she said, 'be angry if you like, but you can't deny you married me on the rebound.'

His lips twisted. 'After eighteen months? Hardly a rebound.'

'Well then, why did you marry me? You told that reporter you'd never marry.'

His eyes wandered over her, noting the dust-smeared tee-shirt, the attractive shape beneath it, the trim waistline and slim hips. With an indolent smile he reached out and stroked a breast. It was a possessive action designed in the circumstances to annoy.

'Propinquity—nearness—is a potent activator of lustful feelings. I wanted a female. Remember I'd lived a celibate life for a long, long time. You were there, a lovely attractive young woman. I wanted you. I knew that the only way I could get you was to marry you. True?'

His caresses were arousing her to such a pitch of excitement she could not stand it. With both of her hands she seized his wrist and threw it from her.

'I hate you, Macaire Delaney, I hate you! I wish I'd never come here. I wish I'd never found you. That photograph on my wall—it's a lie, a great big lie. I w-wish I'd never married you. I'd rather have the dream than the man!'

She ran sobbing from the room.

Half an hour later, Olivia emerged from the bedroom, her face pale and tear-stained, her hair untidy. Mac was making the lunch. When she entered the kitchen he turned and put down the knife he was holding.

'Salad and cold meat,' he said. 'I hope that suits your taste?'

For a moment she was silent, then, 'I'm not hungry.'

Their eyes did battle, then he laughed and walked over to her. 'You hate me, do you, my little sleeping partner? Show how much you hate me. Go on, hit me, scratch me, bite me. Get it out of your system. Then I'll show you how much I hate you.'

She looked up uncertainly, saw a smile twitching and her anger fled. 'Oh, Mac,' she flung her arms round his neck, 'I never know how I'm going to find you. One minute you're my lover, the next you're the hard, embittered man who met me on the doorstep when I first arrived, I don't know how to cope with you.'

His arm went round her waist. 'If you'd wanted a stolid, solid, placid man as a husband——'

'Like Daniel Watling.' At Mac's puzzled frown she explained, 'the man who asked me to marry him.'

'Too bad he lost out to me,' was the sarcastic response. 'If,' Mac continued, 'you'd wanted a life partner like that, you shouldn't have chosen me. I'm as mercurial in my moods as the rest of my kind. Like them, I possess an artistic temperament which has to be reckoned with. It won't go away. You're stuck with it, sweetheart, for as long as you're my wife.'

For as long as you're my wife ... The words both puzzled and frightened her. Did he foresee an end to their marriage?

'Mac, kiss me, Mac,' she whispered.

'You're a shameless hussy,' he murmured, pulling her urgently towards him. He kissed her and it was not until a long time later that their meal was eaten.

It was Raff's wild barking that had Olivia drying her hands from washing the dishes and following Mac to the entrance door. A middle-aged woman was propping her bicycle against the wall and picking her way over the puddles. She was grey-haired and thin and smiling. On her shoulder swung a bag.

'I'm Mrs Appleby, wife of the village postmaster and storekeeper. I've brought you some photographs. You are Mr Connal, aren't you, sir, Mr Macaire Connal?' She did not wait for an answer. 'And Mrs Connal. D'you know, Mr Connal, I've never been so surprised in my life, nor has my husband, to know we had such a famous person living in our village. Well, near it, anyway.'

'My name is Delaney,' Mac said curtly.

'Yes, well,' said Mrs Appleby, 'you're living here at Atherley's Farm, so it couldn't be anyone else, could it? You asked Mr Worth, the photographer, to send these care of the village post office and that's us, so I thought I'd do you a favour and bring them.'

'That's very kind of you, Mrs Appleby,' Olivia said faintly. 'Won't you come in?'

'Thanks, love, but I won't stay. I must congratulate you both on your marriage, though. Lovely pictures they are.'

'How do you know?' Mac again, speaking abruptly. 'Anyway, they should be addressed to Delaney, not Connal.'

'Well, they are, sir, but it's in the local evening paper, you see. I've brought you a couple of copies of the paper, one for each of you. No charge. Well, it was such an important occasion, wasn't it, you getting married, sir? And just think, no one would have known if Mr Ivens hadn't been there to interview that beauty queen. He's a reporter, you see, for the *Moorland Evening Herald*, so he got an exclusive story, he said. He acted as a witness at your marriage, didn't he? Lucky man, if I may say so, Mr—and Mrs—Connal—I mean, Delaney! It says in the article Mr Ivens wrote that you've been missing for a long time, Mr Connal. Nobody knew where you were, even your manager. You disappeared, it says, after you left hospital to convalesce and——'

'It's kind of you, Mrs Appleby,' Mac cut in. 'Thank you for bringing the papers and the photographs.'

She drew another copy of the paper from her bag. 'You couldn't, I suppose, just autograph this lovely picture of you both, could you, Mr Connal? Just write your name—you know, Macaire Connal—across it?' She handed him a pen. 'Oh, thank you, Mr Connal—er—Delaney. That's made my two-mile cycle ride worthwhile.'

As she walked her bicycle through the puddles, she waved and wished them every happiness.

Mac closed the door. He looked at his wife. There was no light in his eyes now. 'It's out,' he said. 'My sanctuary's gone. From now on, I might as well be living in a goldfish bowl.'

His look seemed so accusing, Olivia cried out, 'It's not my fault! You didn't have to marry me. You told me why you did—because you wanted a woman. You implied that every woman had her price and that mine was marriage, so you married me. So how can I be blamed for your hideout being discovered? *I* didn't ask a man who was a reporter to act as one of our witnesses.'

'Have you finished?' he said quietly. She was silent, her eyes carrying on the somewhat one-sided argument. 'I'm going for a walk.' He shrugged on his sheepskin-lined jacket and pushed his feet into boots, pushing the legs of his jeans into them.

Raff, hearing familiar noises, scampered into the room, sat on his haunches and looked expectantly up at his master. 'Not you,' Mac said to the dog.

'Why not?' Olivia asked. 'He'd love to go for a walk.'

'Then take him yourself. I'm leaving him with you mainly because I want to be alone—and I mean alone—in order to think. He'll act as your watchdog. I may be out a long time.'

She began to panic. 'How long, Mac? Where are you going?'

'Across the moors. I don't know how long. For God's sake, don't pester me!'

'But suppose a mist comes down, like the one the other day? You might get lost.'

He gave her an unfathomable look and slammed the door behind him. Raff whined and barked until long after the heavy footsteps had died away.

Olivia did take Raff for a walk. She wandered along the winding road, edged each side by drystone walls that stretched to the limits of the fertile moorland. Above that line the fells rose, grey and forbidding, as remote in their awesome heights as the man she had married. He, too, had risen to awesome heights of world-wide fame and he carried with him, all the time, a remoteness with which she could not even hope to make contact.

She had told him in her anger that she would rather have the picture of him than himself in reality. She had been wrong. It was the man she wanted, to be hers and hers alone. The dream belonged to millions.

Mac had not returned by nightfall. Olivia, miserable, anxious, cooked a meal for two, but it was eaten by one. In the end, she gave Mac's portion to Raff.

It was pointless waiting up for him. It was equally pointless, she discovered when lying in bed, to try to sleep. Her anxiety burned her like a fever. Would he stay out all night?

When a door opened, closed and was locked, when an excited dog ran and scuffled, barking and barking, she knew a relief which left her limp. Footsteps mounted the stairs, water ran into the bath. Eventually, the footsteps came down and the bedroom door opened and closed. Mac had come back to her.

She lay stiffly until the bed sagged under his weight, then she turned on to her side away from him. He lay on his back, arm on the pillow under his head. By the uneven tempo of his breathing she knew that, like herself, he was awake. Would his thinking go on all night? Hadn't he thought enough? Olivia stirred restlessly, punching her pillow, pulling at the bedclothes, moving her hair from her eyes.

With a hard hand he pulled her round.

'If my fidgeting annoys you,' she mumbled, 'I can't help it. I want to fidget and I'm going to keep on fidgeting.'

It sounded childish, but she could not stay silent any longer.

'Who's arguing?' was his laconic reply. Almost casually, as if he were motivated by marital rights rather than emotions, he moved until their bodies touched lightly.

He pulled at her pyjama jacket collar. 'So our prim little miss is back? I'll make short work of that.' And he did, unfastening the buttons in spite of her hands which tried to stop him, pushing the jacket from her shoulders and arms and caressing her lingeringly until her body moved of its own volition to press against his.

He gave a low, exultant laugh and soon her entire body was bereft of covering. He covered her with kisses, his caressing hand gentle now, then savagely demanding, as if anger was, as usual, not far away. As their limbs entwined and their mouths sought each other's hungrily, Olivia gave of herself more completely than ever before. She submitted, she demanded, she provoked, she acquiesced, she laughed, arching herself towards him and almost crying with joy as her body surrendered at last to his hard male dominance and conquest.

Afterwards they lay, still locked in embrace, while the ecstasy died to a contented throb, and never had they been so entirely as one.

'Oh, Mac,' she said at last, stroking his hair, 'I thought you'd left me. I thought I'd never see you again.'

'You married a complex man, my darling,' he murmured, burying his face in her neck. 'I wanted solitude in those hours. It's something I've needed constantly in the past, and will need many times in the future.' She could find no answer. 'I made a phone call,' he added.

She wanted to ask, who was it you phoned? The woman who left you? Someone from your past life? But she could ask nothing. Contentment and exhaustion had claimed him. He was asleep. Anyway, she thought, surrendering slowly to sleep herself, he would never have told me, even if I had asked.

There was a hammering on the door. Raff almost barked himself hoarse. Mac surfaced first, cursing and searching for some kind of clothing.

'Who is it, Mac?' Olivia asked drowsily.

'I don't know, but whoever it is can get the hell out of here. Stay where you are, I'll be back.' He dressed, zipping the front of his jeans and tugging a polo-necked sweater over his shirt.

There were voices in the large room, and it was plain that Mac knew the caller. They were arguing. Mac was angry, furiously so. Whoever could stand up to Mac in such a mood, Olivia thought, smiling, must have a skin like an elephant's hide. Less sense than an elephant, too, because such an intelligent animal would have turned and run at such a spate of expletives and curses.

The caller was recognisably male. And still he stood his ground. Olivia heard the raised voice ask,

'Well, where is this damned female you've been crazy enough to get yourself hitched to? Couldn't you have been content to live with the girl?'

Olivia thrust aside the bedclothes, pulled on underwear, jeans and shirt and ran a comb through her hair. As she approached the room, she heard the visitor say, 'Annetta's in circulation again. She's getting a divorce. Now there's a woman for you! From what she says, she's willing to continue your relationship from where it left off. She's been asking about you.'

'How kind of her,' was Mac's sarcastic reply.

'Good morning.' At the sound of Olivia's voice the two men swung round. She offered her hand to the stranger. 'I'm the "damned female" Mac's been crazy enough to marry. I hope I'm being more polite to our visitor than you are being to your hostess.'

The visitor had the grace to turn red. He took the proffered hand, shaking it briefly. He was tall and grey-haired. His face was narrow with prominent cheekbones, his eyes darting, his body thin.

'I'm Mac's wife,' Olivia continued. She turned wide, questioning eyes to Mac's. 'Who———?'

He answered curtly, 'Fulton, Fulton Hallinger. My manager, public relations man and promoter of my public image. Fulton, my wife, Olivia.'

The man's eyes skimmed with distaste over Olivia's slim figure. 'Pardon me, Mrs Delaney.' The man spoke without sincerity. 'I didn't realise———'

'That I was within earshot? For a public relations man, Mr Hallinger, that was a bad mistake. Surely you know how it is when two people in love are on their honeymoon? They can hardly bear to be apart.' She took Mac's left hand in hers and saw Fulton's eyes widen in alarm.

'Be careful,' he said anxiously. 'That's his damaged———'

Deliberately she put her other hand on Mac's left arm. Fulton Hallinger winced. 'Mr Hallinger seems to have a lot of jobs, darling,' she said, looking artlessly up at her husband. 'One of them appears to be to get us divorced almost before the ink has dried on our marriage certificate.' Her voice wavered, then steadied. 'After only two days of ecstatically happy marriage, that's asking rather a lot of us, isn't it, Mr Hallinger? But if having a wife is going to ruin Mac's public image, I'll get into my car out there and drive out of his life. Just say the word and I'll——'

'Shut up, you little fool. Fulton, would you get the hell out of here?'

'I want an answer, Macaire.'

Olivia touched Macaire's shoulder. 'Mac?'

'Can't you guess?' was the bitter reply. 'He's pressurising me to return to civilisation, have treatment on my arm and take up my career from where it literally came to a crash stop. The answer's "no", Fulton. Sorry. You didn't have to come all this way—I told you on the phone.'

So now she knew to whom he had made that phone call. She also knew why, but questions remained. 'When you went out for your walk, Mac,' Olivia probed, 'you knew the report about our marriage was in the local paper, which meant that only the people in the surrounding districts would read about you. So why, if you didn't want to go back to your old life, did you contact Mr Hallinger?'

Macaire sighed shortly. 'It was in the national dailies, too. I saw them on sale in the general store when I walked through the village. That damned reporter Ivens got his money's worth from my reappearance. He must have called all the national papers he could think of and got paid by all of them for the story.'

'It made the headlines in some of the papers,' Fulton said. 'If you hadn't called me, Macaire, I was going to move heaven and earth to find you.'

'Which is why I called you—to save you the trouble.'

Fulton Hallinger shook his head. 'Waste of money. You didn't really think I'd let you slip through my fingers a second time, did you?'

'But Mac,' Olivia said, pleading with her eyes, 'I can't understand why you're refusing. It would be wonderful to hear you play again. I've already told you how——'

'How much you long to hear me,' her husband cut in sarcastically. 'You see, Fulton, whether you like it or not, my wife's on your side. So regard her as a friend instead of an enemy. She's a fan of mine. That's something the reporter missed. Think of the headline that never was—She

Married the Man of Her Dreams.'

Fulton Hallinger's eyes gleamed unpleasantly. 'Okay, so I've got an ally in the highest places, so to speak. I think I can now get the hell out of here, as you so politely put it. I'm sure your *lovely* wife,' with a falsely courteous bow, 'will use her persuasive powers and do my work for me much better than I could myself. By the way, dear,' to Olivia, 'drop the "Mac", will you? It's bad for his image. Call him Macaire, like everyone else.'

'She'll call me what the hell she likes. You haven't landed your fish yet, Hallinger. I could twist and turn on the end of your line and make my escape——' Mac turned blazing eyes on to his bewildered wife, 'from both of you.'

CHAPTER SIX

'WHAT was that supposed to mean?' Olivia confronted her husband, her face pale. They were alone again after Fulton Hallinger's departure.

'The words,' Mac replied coldly, 'were surely self-explanatory.'

Olivia responded, her voice rising, 'I could "make my escape", too. I could, as I said, get in my car and drive out of your life. You know about me only what I've chosen to tell you. You wouldn't find me. A divorce could be arranged, then you could have this Annetta who seems to be willing to return to you. She could marry you and take away all your bitterness against life—and women. Is that what you want?' she persisted. 'For me to go?'

It became plain that he was not going to reply.

'You're looking at me as if I were a traitor!' she cried. 'What do you expect of me? To lie and say I don't care if you never play another note, that I don't ever want to hear you perform at the piano again?'

Their eyes met, his dark and fathomless, hers brilliant with suppressed tears. He said, as if the subject wearied him, 'Let's get some breakfast.'

Fulton Hallinger's visit had had a disastrous effect on Mac's mood. Gone was the closeness which their love-making had created. He had turned back into the aloof stranger, withdrawn into a world which she could never hope to glimpse, let alone be welcomed into.

After breakfast, Olivia watched Mac push his feet into boots and tuck his jeans into the tops. 'Where are you going?' she asked tonelessly. 'For another of your interminable walks?'

'What's wrong with that?'

She glanced out of the window, seeing the wide, rolling moorland painted pale yellow with the early spring sunshine. 'Nothing, except that I would like to go for a walk, too.'

'What's stopping you?'

'You can't really mean that you would go one way while I went another?' Even as she asked the question, she knew his answer.

'You'll have to learn, as my wife, that I need my solitude as much as others need people around them.'

'That's an extremely selfish attitude.'

'Selfish or not, that's my way. Take it or leave it.'

She watched him to the door. 'You can't honestly mean you'd go and leave me alone again for hours as you did the other day?'

He turned towards her. 'You don't like solitude? You're one of the other kind? You don't like your own company?'

'Would I have taken myself off on vacation alone if I didn't?' His face remained hard. 'We can be alone together, Mac. Take me with you, and I'll prove it.'

'I require no proof. Your presence would distract me. I'd be conscious of you all the time. With you by my side, it would be impossible for me to think deeply.'

Her heart sank and she turned hopelessly away. 'I'll know better next time than to try to force my company on you.'

He made no loving, encouraging comment in return. Instead he said, 'When you found me here, I was alone, except for Raff.'

'And you don't have to converse with him.'

'Thank God, no. Look, Olivia,' she faced him and her heart hit the bottom at his serious tone, 'you must have known when you agreed to become my wife that a marriage certificate could only give you certain legal rights, that you couldn't buy me with it. You knew from the moment we met that I was a hermit at heart, a recluse, a loner.'

'But,' she said, bewildered, 'when we make love, we become *one*, Mac, one person, intellectually and physically. We—we fuse into each other. I become part of you. I'm trying—not very well—to tell you that I understand your needs because I'm made that way myself. If only you would let me into your world———'

'Stay out of my world, woman. There's none who can share it, neither man nor woman.'

She swung from him again, compressing her lips to control their trembling. He was turning her away just as surely as he turned her away from the farmhouse the day she arrived, and the day after that.

At the door he said, 'Either accept the fact, Olivia, or leave. Now, before any emotional complications arise. I'm fireproof in that respect but, since you're a woman, you are not. So, as you said earlier, there's your car. Repack your cases and go. It's your choice.'

'Mac!' she cried after him as he closed the door. She wrenched it open again. 'Mac!' she shrieked as she watched him picking his way across the muddy farmyard. 'I didn't mean it. I'll never leave you, I promise . . .'

Only the dog answered, barking frenziedly.

Olivia raced up the stairs, turned the key which was still in the lock of Mac's private room and flung herself inside.

Since her aunt had owned a hi-fi system, it did not take long for Olivia to work out how to operate Mac's. Without a moment's hesitation, she pulled from the rack a record which displayed on its cover a profile of her husband's face.

For a long moment she gazed at it. Once she would have smiled and playfully pressed the picture close, then held it at a distance and admired the image of the man. She would have sighed over the fine features which pulled at her heartstrings, at the sensitive lips, the unfathomable eyes, worshipping him from afar . . . Knowing and accepting that the dreams her fantasies wove around him could never come true.

Now she was intimately acquainted with the man beyond the image, having learned about him all he would allow her to learn—and the useless tears tore at her throat. Inside, he was as hard and roughly-hewn as a newly-mined diamond. All his tenderness, delicacy and sensitivity were reserved totally for his music.

If her love did not move him, then what good would it do

to cry? What use would tears be in persuading him to allow her to share his own private world?

There was an armchair placed centrally between the speakers. The sound of his playing, perfection itself, the music which had come from the mind of the composer passing through the pianist's and being interpreted by him, gave her a pleasure it was impossible to describe.

After the record had finished, she found another and another, all recordings made in the past by Macaire Connal. If she could not have his companionship or his love, at least she could have his music. She would get drunk with it, drown herself in it . . . She did not care any more whether or not he objected. He could not deny her——

The door swung open and a man with blazing eyes stood rigidly in the doorway. 'Who gave you permission,' he rasped, 'to use my hi-fi system? Who told you you could play my records? Who said you had right of access to this room whenever you choose?'

Questions, hurled at her but which demanded no answer. They were an expression of anger so fierce she floundered and almost sank. His arrival and attack, catching her at one of her most vulnerable moments, when physical feeling had been suspended and emotions had taken over, had made his onslaught all the more devastating. She could find no words with which to answer him. Nor, when he strode in with Raff at his heels, could she move to stop him as he switched off the hi-fi equipment, snatched the record from the turntable and hurled it to the other side of the room.

'Mac!' she shrieked, her face white, her eyes staring, 'what have you done? It was you—*you* playing at your utmost best.' She raced across and pulled the record from behind the roll-top desk where it had fallen.

It was damaged beyond use, but she held it to her breast, coveting it, protecting it. But the ferocity of his anger seemed to have been allayed by his violent action.

There was, however, no remorse in him for what he had done. He smiled cynically. 'You're putting on an excellent act. But then it's all in a "good" cause, isn't it? It's your way of contributing to the "bring back Macaire Connal" campaign. You want me to return to the limelight,' he accused, 'for the same reason as my manager—for the money to be got out of my reinstatement as one of the world's top concert pianists.'

Olivia tried shaking her head, but she might have saved herself the bother.

'It won't be long now,' he continued bitterly, 'before representatives of my recording company arrive on the doorstep. Hallinger will tell them where I am. Then the publicity machine will grind into action, and I'll be minced into little pieces as I was before. When I found this haven, broken down though it was, I had begun to put myself together again—almost succeeded, in fact. Then you came out of the mist to torment me and now I'm right back where I was.'

Raff had flopped down, nose on paws, but his eyes were watchful. It was as if he knew things were wrong, that his future was being decided as much as those of his two human companions.

The tears which had been locked in Olivia's throat fought their way into her eyes. 'I listened to your records,' she said thickly, 'for my own pleasure. For escape, if you like, from the impossible position you've forced me into. You've labelled me an accomplice, and I'm under no illusion— nothing I say will shift your opinion of my motives.'

He peeled off his jacket and flung it down. His boots had made mud-stains on the thin bronze-patterned carpet.

'I'm not after your money,' she whispered. 'I don't need your money.' As his eyebrows lifted, she said hastily, 'I don't need money. I can live quite happily without it, if need be. But Mac, don't you understand—if you continue to ignore that wonderful gift you have, all that music inside you will turn sour. It will have to make its way out some time. Better that the realisation should come now, while you're young, than when you're old and full of regrets. If you make no attempt at a comeback now, you'll never forgive yourself for the rest of your life.'

His arms were folded across his chest. He had heard her out with a smile, a sardonic one. 'Where has a young, untried woman learnt such wisdom, such worldly knowledge? If you really have spent ten years tied to an ailing aunt, experience could hardly have been your teacher.'

'Don't doubt my honesty,' she snapped. 'What I told you about my life was the truth. My aunt was my teacher. She spoke to me often of her own life, her regrets about her undeveloped talents, her missed opportunities. I didn't shut my ears to her stories as some young people might have done. I listened and absorbed and stored the information away in my mind.'

'You enthrall me with your tales,' he commented. 'But they haven't fooled me, my sweet. I still believe you're after what you can get out of me, like all the others.'

Infuriated by his intractability, she sent the useless disc spinning through the air towards him. He stood his ground. The disc hit him just below the eye and she gasped at what she had done.

'Mac,' she choked, 'oh, God, I didn't mean——!' She ran to him, saw the blood running from the graze, flung her arms round his neck and put her lips to the wound.

He tore her away and threw her from him. Olivia noticed, distressed though she was, that he had used his left arm.

'Pack your things,' he commanded. 'We're leaving.' He turned and went along the landing.

'Where are we going?' she called after him frantically. 'What about all the food, the broken windows, the furniture? Anybody could get in and vandalise the lot.'

At the head of the stairs he turned. 'Why the hell should I care? Even less, you. *I* found this sanctuary and nurtured it. In turn it nurtured me. *You* were the unwanted invader.'

'Mac,' she cried after his retreating form, 'I'm your wife . . .'

Raff went scurrying after him.

There was not much for Olivia to pack. Some instinct must have prevented her from emptying her suitcases after the wedding ceremony.

It seemed that Mac had little more to pack than herself.

Most of it he seemed intent on leaving behind, even the expensive hi-fi system. 'I've got better equipment in my home,' he said carelessly when she questioned him.

'Is that where we're going?'

He nodded and asked her if she was capable of driving south to Surrey.

'Easily,' she answered, 'especially as I came from farther south than that. From Sussex,' she added, and waited for further questions. None came, and she wondered why. She felt it was time to tell him of her own circumstances, but still something restrained her. Was it that this marriage to Macaire Connal still possessed the substance of a dream and that her unconscious mind refused to accept it as reality?

The drive was long and tiring. It had been late afternoon before they left. Raff lay curled on the back seat, sleeping deeply. Olivia envied the dog his ability to switch off from life's problems. She longed to have that ability, to turn off her physical tiredness and the strange creeping despair which was taking over from her habitual optimism, and sleep and sleep ... waking to find herself wrapped about by Mac's arms.

Those arms were at that moment folded across his chest as he sat, with the impatience of a man used to taking charge and irritated by being forced to be a passive passenger. Olivia secretly wondered at the apparently increasing mobility of his damaged arm and pleasure leapt inside her at the thought.

They stopped now and then for Raff, for food, for shopping and for petrol. It was past midnight when they arrived in the county of Surrey. Mac directed her to turn right into a drive which, he said, led to his house. It was a narrow drive but widened as it progressed.

The house took Olivia's breath away. It was a small country mansion and it gleamed white in the moonlit darkness.

'You must be exhausted,' said Mac. 'Come on, woman, out of there. We both of us need sleep. You, too, hound.' Raff leapt across to the front seat and out of the car. Olivia looked around for a garage, then locked the doors. 'It will be safe here until morning,' Mac told her.

He took her cases from the car and handed them to her, apologising for being unable to carry them. He extracted his own case and led the way. Raff, tail wagging madly, knew that he too had come home. He searched out old haunts, raced madly from bush to tree to ornamental pond and back to base.

Mac unlocked the front door, stood aside and motioned to Olivia to enter. She looked at him, trying in the darkness to gauge his mood. 'You should,' she said, smiling, 'carry me over the threshold.'

There was a brittle silence, then she covered her mouth, realising her blunder.

'It would be my greatest pleasure,' Mac answered frigidly, 'to do just that. One day, however, I promise that I shall do so.'

'I'm sorry, Mac.'

'Forget it. Please go in.' He whistled to his dog, who pushed past them and was first inside.

If the outside of the building had startled Olivia, the interior made her gasp. It revealed beyond any doubt the extent of the wealth which her husband's fame had brought him.

'Aren't you glad you married me?' he taunted, watching her face. 'Aren't you pleased, now, that you gambled with fate and joined your life to that of the tattered, bearded, long-haired recluse you stumbled upon accidentally, and whom you nursed so gallantly back to health in that decaying farmhouse on the Yorkshire moors?'

'I'm glad I married him,' she responded quietly, 'even though his personality is as embittered and disagreeable now he's dressed in conventional clothes as he was when dressed in rags.'

'Thanks,' he said sarcastically. 'My home awaits you, my darling wife. Look on it as belonging to both of us from this moment on and until death us do part.'

She stumbled over the step and his right hand shot out to steady her.

'Are you drunk with delight at what you see?' he said. 'Are you so eager to get a possessive foot inside the door that you're falling over yourself to take up residence?'

Olivia jerked irritably from the hand that still held her arm. She gave him a furious look. 'I think I liked you better in that old farmhouse after all.'

He smiled but his eyes stayed cold. 'I doubt if you mean that.' He closed the door and led her into a large, high-ceilinged room. The furniture, the decor, the ornaments, the paintings . . . in her exhausted state she held them mentally from her, refusing to acknowledge their existence. She sank into the nearest chair.

'Can't you take it, my love?' Macaire asked mockingly. 'Is the contrast between your cramped bed-sit in the attic of some Victorian house and this,' his right arm lifted in a sweeping motion, 'too much for you to take in all at once?'

'Bed-sit?' she asked, emerging momentarily from her dazed state.

'Since you must live somewhere, I assumed that a girl like you, without employment, would be forced to live somewhere relatively cheap. Was I wrong?'

Her head sank with fatigue. 'I have a house to live in.' He did not respond, so she assumed he wanted some explanation. 'My aunt left it to me.' At all costs, she told herself she mustn't give away too much of her secret. 'A small house, nothing special, really. It was very kind of her.'

'Didn't she have any other close relatives, grandchildren or——'

'I was her closest relative. She was my mother's sister, I told you. My aunt was not married.'

He seemed deep in thought and had made no move to show her to a bedroom.

'Please, Macaire, I'm very tired. Can I go to bed?'

He frowned, appeared to hesitate, then said, 'Follow me.'

In the entrance hall, he picked up one of her suitcases while she gripped the other. His left arm, she noticed, lifted slowly—and not without pain—to rest in his pocket. 'Will the beds be made?' she asked, a stair or two behind him. 'The house feels warm, too.'

'I have a housekeeper. She lives at the lodge we passed at the start of the drive. You were driving, so you may not have noticed it. Her husband is there, too, of course, and he works for me in other ways.'

'So she's looked after the house in your absence?'

They had reached the landing and Olivia glanced to the right and left, wondering which way he would go.

'She had instructions to do so.'

'How did she know when you'd be back?'

'She didn't, any more than I did. When you meet her in the morning, my sudden acquisition of a wife will probably make her faint dead away.'

She turned from his sardonic smile. 'I'm sorry I'm such an embarrassment to you.'

He turned right and she followed him again. 'Embarrassment?' he murmured when she had caught him up. 'My darling, you've become an absolute necessity to me.' They stopped outside a door. 'Physiologically speaking, of course.'

Her flaring eyes amused him. He opened the door and went into the room. There were twin beds. A bathroom door stood open. A tiny vase of spring flowers, newly-picked, adorned the small dressing-table. Between the beds was a small cabinet on which stood a table lamp and an ashtray. On a shelf below were magazines.

'I apologise for welcoming home my bride by accommodating her in a guest room,' he said, 'but I very much doubt if my own suite of rooms has been made ready for two.'

'I don't mind,' said Olivia, looking round and minding very much indeed. 'It's a lovely room. I'll be fine here.'

'Good.' He put down her case and went out.

Not even goodnight, she thought, trying to swallow the lump in her throat. Some homecoming! She gazed out at the darkness, seeing nothing.

'I forgot to ask.' He had come back. She turned, hoping he would not see the tears. 'Would you like a hot drink? Food?' She shook her head. He studied her closely for a few moments and she said hurriedly,

'A quick shower and I'll be hitting the pillow. Thanks all the same.'

Fifteen minutes later she was in bed, the one nearest the window. As she turned to switch off the table lamp, Macaire came in. 'Raff kept me,' he said. 'A couple of times round the house was not enough for him.' He closed the door. 'Mrs Faber's husband usually takes him, but I can't get them up at this late hour.'

He started to strip and Olivia's face turned pink. At the farmhouse their shared intimacies had seemed so natural. Here, in more civilised surroundings, with every possible convenience she could wish for, it was more like the first night of marriage to a stranger.

He tugged at the catch of the belt around the waistband of his slacks and she said quickly, 'You're sleeping in here?'

He frowned. 'Why not? Do you object?'

'No, no, but——' Her eyes roamed lovingly over his torso, remembering the way he had crushed her to that hard chest in the past week, how his arm had held her fast, how her finger had traced that handsome profile, how . . .

'But what?' He had moved to her bedside and stood over her, eyes glinting. He bent down, supporting himself on his right hand, and she caught the aroma of his maleness, saw the muscles in his shoulder line, the tough leanness of his waist above the loosened belt.

He pulled down the bedclothes from her chin and saw, with a glance of disgust, that she wore pyjamas, buttoned to her neck. 'Virginal and coy tonight, are we?'

She snatched the bedclothes high again and turned on to her side. 'I'm tired,' she snapped, and closed her eyes tightly.

'Me, too, my precious,' he said with an ironic smile, 'so you're safe from my carnal desires tonight.'

There was the running of water from the bathroom, the clink of objects on a glass shelf. When he returned his robe was over his arm and he was wearing nothing. She could not explain the shock it gave her to see him naked, nor could she quell the quick rush of desire which fountained within her own body at the sight.

At last the light was switched off but, tired though she was, Olivia could not relax. Even after only a week of marriage, she had grown used to the feel of him beside her, of hearing his breathing on the pillow next to hers. Now he was not there, she felt as though a piece of her had been lost and she wanted it back.

'Will you come here?' The order came roughly through the darkness. 'I'm missing your body as much as you're missing mine.' He waited a moment, then said huskily, 'Come to me, my lovely.' It was exhaustion making him so tender, she told herself, his driving male need of a female beside him.

Nevertheless she had crossed the dividing space in three seconds and was manoeuvring herself into the narrow bed beside him. He pulled her against him as if absorbing the very essence of her into him. 'That's better,' he sighed. Already he was drifting into sleep. 'How can I tell you how much I need you?' The words were slurring one into the other.

To whom was he speaking, she agonised, herself or that woman he had called to in his fever when she had nursed him through the night? Oh, what did it matter? she sighed. I'm the one he married. I, Olivia Delaney, am his wife. I'm his, every small part of me, whether he wants me or not. Then she too was deeply asleep, entwined in his arms.

When she awoke, the body-clock inside her told her it was late. She needed to wash, she needed to dress and she wanted breakfast. Most of all, she wanted to find her husband.

Soon she was ready, dressed in beige slacks and a white shirt-blouse. After the dampness and chill of the farmhouse, the house seemed almost tropically warm.

Outside the bedroom she felt lost. The landing, with its many doors opening off, stretched right and left and turned corners. Since one man could not possibly occupy all this space, Olivia concluded that her husband must have been in the habit of entertaining frequently. With his professed love of solitude, however, the idea of his liking his fellow human beings well enough to invite them for long weekends was difficult to accept.

On her way down the long, curving flight of stairs, richly carpeted and leading to the extensive entrance hall, she heard Macaire's voice raised and irritable.

'Can't I be allowed to have a few days' peace even in my own home? Who told you I was here, anyway? You guessed, from what the newspapers said? How the hell did the press know about my movements?' A short silence, then, 'A reporter called Peter Ivens found the farmhouse empty and drew conclusions which happened to be correct? And as a result, no doubt, he again made a minor fortune by informing the national dailies. Look, Fulton, I want a day or two's peace. Just leave me alone, will you? Yes, I'm exercising my arm at last, as the doctor told me to do a year ago. It's coming on—slowly.'

Olivia heard the heavy sigh as she opened Macaire's door. 'Here's my wife, Fulton. I must go.' A pause. 'Get *rid* of her? What the——? Get her out of my life? Man, you must be crazy!' He slammed the receiver down and swung round in the office-type chair. He had been seated at a desk.

He stared at her and it was the stranger on the doorstep again. Where was the tenderness he had shown her in the night? But even as he had murmured the endearments, hadn't she known in her heart that he wasn't talking to her? Now he was looking at her as if he had never seen her in his life before.

'Peter Ivens?' she queried faintly. 'I heard what you said.'

'That damned witness at our wedding, no less.'

'But, Macaire, why are you fighting against what will be, what *must* be? You know in your heart that one day you'll play again. Not just because the public wants to hear you, but because of something inside yourself driving you——'

'My God,' he rose, 'with a nagging conscience-prodder like you around, I certainly don't need Fulton Hallinger. If he knew how persistently you were doing his work for him, he wouldn't have told me to——' He stopped, looking at her.

'I heard,' she said bitterly. 'Get me out of your life.' To hide her trembling lips she swung from him. 'Where's the kitchen?'

His hand came out, fastening on to her upper arm, turning her back. 'Mrs Faber's in there. She's cooking us breakfast.'

'I'm not hungry. I was, but my appetite's gone.'

'What's biting you, woman? Didn't you hear the answer I gave Hallinger?'

'I did, but by then you knew I was in the room.'

He pushed her arm from him and went to the window. There was a long silence. To break it, Olivia asked, 'Where's Raff?'

Macaire shrugged. 'Out somewhere in the grounds. They're quite extensive, like the house. I must show you round some time.'

She asked tonelessly, 'Why did you buy such a big house? There are so many rooms I can't believe it. Do you really entertain on the lavish scale the number of bedrooms suggest?'

He gave another exasperated sigh and continued to gaze at the view. 'The house was not entirely my choice. My former fiancée, Annetta, decided it would make a suitable background for us both. Two famous people, she said. We couldn't live in a rabbit hutch. We just had to have visitors, it would be expected of us. Just as long as she left me alone to my music, I let her get on with it. Money was no object, since we both had a surplus of the stuff. With your liking for music, maybe you've heard of her—Annetta Brambella?'

'I read about her in those press cuttings you'd kept. I would have thought,' she said dully, 'you'd have made an ideal couple.'

'So did the world of music. So did Fulton Hallinger. So did the world's press. Everyone except Annetta. As you may have discovered from those cuttings, she ran off with someone else three days before our wedding.'

'Which means this house still belongs to both of you?'

'I haven't really thought about it. Too many dramatic happenings piled one on the other at the time and put the whole subject out of my mind. She married someone else.'

'Now she's divorcing him. So——?' What about the house, she meant. The knowledge that half of the house he called his own might still belong to his ex-fiancée was disturbing. It made her feel a stranger in her husband's home. 'The house is beautiful,' she said.'

'You like it?' The tone revealed his own indifference. 'No doubt to you, with your modest upbringing and poverty-haunted environment, it's a palace.'

She smiled secretly at his assumptions about her background.

The telephone rang. Macaire made no move to answer it, so Olivia said, 'Shall I?' and lifted the receiver. 'Macaire Connal's residence.'

'Mrs Faber?' It was the voice of someone she had come to dislike intensely.

'No. This is Mr Connal's wife. Who is that, please?'

'Fulton Hallinger. Where's Macaire?'

Olivia took offence at the tone. 'He's . . .' She paused and asked warily, 'Why do you want to speak to him, Mr Hallinger?'

'Listen, Mrs Delaney, I'm his manager. What I have to say to him is his business and mine. Now, for Pete's sake, cut out this interrogation and put me on to him.'

Olivia pressed a hand over the mouthpiece. 'Did you hear?' Macaire nodded. 'Do you want to speak to him?' He mouthed a 'No.' 'Mr Hallinger? My husband is busy at the moment. I'm afraid——'

'Look, darling, I know damned well he's in the same room as you. I'm not one of your media men you can brush off like a piece of dirt. So put him on to me, will you?'

Olivia said, with the mouthpiece a hand's span from her lips, 'Mac, tell your manager from me that he could do with polishing up his telephone manner. In my opinion, as a public relations man he's about as effective as a hippopotamus in a rabbit hutch!'

Macaire gave one shout of laughter and took the receiver. 'That's put you in your place, my friend.'

Olivia heard a string of invective, followed by the words,

clearly spoken, 'Tell her from me she's a high-handed, supercilious, highfalutin' little bitch.'

'No need to tell her. She's heard and she's fighting mad. I told you before, Fulton, she's really on your side.' He listened. 'You'd rather have the three witches from *Macbeth* on your side?' He looked at his wife. 'Got that, darling? My manager doesn't like you.' Olivia murmured some words and Macaire bent to hear them. 'She says she hates your guts, too. So it's friends all round.'

Macaire turned his back on her. 'Annetta's in circulation? You told me. So what? I'm a married man. I wear a ring on my finger, another woman's ring. My wife's.'

Olivia swung out of the room and Macaire did not call her back. She found her way into one room after another. As she noted the elegance and beauty all around her, she wondered whose taste had prevailed in the choice of furniture and decorations—Macaire's or his ex-fiancée's? Since men usually left the buying of such things to their wife-to-be, it was almost certainly Annetta who had chosen everything that had contrived to make the house a showpiece. To Olivia's eyes, it could not be called a home. It was a beautiful stage-setting for two famous people.

In the kitchen, Olivia found Mrs Faber. She introduced herself and the housekeeper seemed delighted to make her acquaintance, a fact which puzzled Olivia. 'We never thought Mr Delaney would marry, my Jack and me,' Mrs Faber said. 'After what he went through with someone who shall be nameless, and then that accident . . .' Mrs Faber eyed her wonderingly. 'Fancy you finding him when he'd shut himself away. No one knew where he'd vanished to.'

Olivia felt Mrs Faber should know the truth. 'When I found him he was very ill,' she said. 'I nursed him back to health. You see, he'd neglected himself terribly.' Mrs Faber tutted, sincerely concerned. 'When he asked me to marry him, Mrs Faber, he didn't tell me who he was. And although I've even got a poster of him on the wall of my room——' she coloured slightly and explained, 'I'm one of his fans,' the housekeeper nodded her greying head as if it were a perfectly natural thing to be a fan of Macaire Connal, 'I didn't recognise him because—well, he had a beard and long hair and holes in his clothes. It wasn't until the marriage ceremony that I knew his true identity.'

'Then I bet you nearly fainted,' said Mrs Faber, her eyes bright and laughing. 'It all sounds so romantic.' Olivia thought of the conditions in which Macaire had been living and smiled at the housekeeper's description. 'So,' Mrs Faber went on, 'it was love at first sight.'

'Yes, oh yes, it was. For—for both of us.' She couldn't spoil Mrs Faber's romantic illusions by treading on her dreams. Mrs Faber sighed contentedly and Macaire's voice said behind them,

'She's telling the most fantastic lies, Mrs Faber.'

Olivia saw the housekeeper's puzzlement and swung round, trying to warn Macaire. 'It was, it was,' she protested. 'On my part, anyway. I know that with you it was different.'

To her sorrow, he did not deny the statement. 'She thought I was a murderer in hiding, Mrs Faber,' Macaire said, his voice hissing with a false menace.

'The villagers thought there was something strange about you, too,' she said defensively.

'She thought,' he went on, ignoring her words, 'that I was going to rape her, then do away with her. I let her think so, then I turned her out into the mist, but she came back. Next morning I turned her out again, and she came back again.'

Olivia's face flamed. 'Because there was nowhere else to go, that's why! He had no heart, Mrs Faber. Would you turn a girl out into a terrible cold mist despite the fact that she might get lost among the moors and hills?' Mrs Faber shook her head. 'Well, he did!' Mrs Faber tutted, as though she couldn't believe it.

In three strides Macaire confronted his wife. His right arm encircled her waist and pulled her close. His mouth claimed hers in a long kiss. When his head lifted, his eyes promised more to come when their audience was not present. 'So why did you marry me?' he asked.

Conscious of the housekeeper's intense interest, Olivia

could only shake her head.

'It's what she told me, Mr Delaney,' said Mrs Faber, 'love at first sight.'

'Ah, but of course!' Macaire's eyes glittered sardonically, yet it seemed he had decided to play along with the housekeeper's belief in their instant attraction for each other. He turned to her. 'I never thought such a girl as this existed, Mrs Faber. The moment she walked into my life, I was so afraid of losing her again,' only Olivia could perceive the mockery in his smile, 'I had to make her mine, truly and legally mine, as soon as I possibly could. She came to me out of the mist, and I was afraid she would disappear back into the mist and out of my life.'

Mrs Faber sighed, satisfied at last to have heard the truth, as she regarded it, from her employer's own lips. 'You two lovebirds make me feel young again,' she said. 'Wait till I tell my Jack. Pretended to be a criminal indeed!' She laughed heartily and her ample body shook. 'Now off with you and I'll bring your breakfast.'

Macaire said with a sly smile, 'My wife told me she wasn't hungry.'

Olivia jerked from his hold. 'Oh, but I am, I'm starving hungry, Mrs Faber!'

At which the housekeeper laughed again and said it was only natural to be hungry at their stage of marriage. 'After all,' she added meaningfully, 'we don't know what Mother Nature holds in store for us, do we?'

Olivia coloured to the roots of her hair and Macaire looked astonished. In the breakfast room he asked, as they took their seats at the table, 'What have you been telling my housekeeper?' His manner had changed to that of the more familiar detached stranger.

'If you're referring to her last remark, that came entirely from her imagination.'

There was a moment's silence, then he said, 'It's something we must consider, nevertheless.'

'You can rest assured,' she said, her voice low, 'that in the circumstances that prevail at this particular point in time, I'll take good care that no child results from our—

our intimate activities.' 'Lovemaking', she had almost said, but it would have made a mockery of the expression.

After a long silence, during which Macaire considered the slowly-flexing fingers of his left hand, he commented, 'Good.' Thus abruptly, the subject of the creation or non-creation of the future generation of Delaneys was dismissed.

Olivia felt near to tears. He had not once asked her whether she wanted children, nor had he told her his own wishes on the subject. All of her remembered life she had accepted that one day she would have a family of her own. She had also decided that, come what may, her own marriage would not break up as her own parents' had.

After breakfast, Macaire said, 'Can you amuse yourself for a while? I have some telephoning to do.' Olivia nodded, then frowned, hoping he would tell her who it was he was calling. He went from the room, having made no explanation.

Olivia returned to the kitchen to collect Raff. He lifted himself from his basket and came happily to greet her. His gold name-tag rattled as he snuffled at her feet. 'I'm going for a walk around the estate,' Olivia told Mrs Faber. 'Should I take a lead for Raff?'

The housekeeper shook her head. 'There's nowhere he could get out. I expect you'll find my Jack busy out there.'

She did indeed find Mrs Faber's husband busy in the grounds. He was digging the earth when Raff bounded up to him, but he bent down to ruffle the dog's fur. 'Good to see you back, boy,' he said. Then he straightened. 'Mrs Delaney? Very happy to meet you, ma'am.' He held out his hand and Olivia placed hers in his hard grip. He was narrow-faced and weather-worn and had contented eyes. It was plain that he loved his work.

'Just loosening the earth in the vegetable patch. Got some carrot seeds to sow and some peas. Mr Delaney does like his home-grown vegetables. But,' he laughed, 'you being his wife now, I expect you know that.'

Olivia did not know that. In fact, she was beginning to discover just how little she did know about her new husband. She talked for a while to Mr Faber, about the surrounding countryside, about the famous Box Hill not far away which was so named because of its ancient box trees. It was, Mr Faber told her, a popular picnic place even in the reign of Charles II in the seventeenth century. She must, he said, persuade her husband to take her there some time. 'You can see for miles up there,' he finished, 'even across to the South Downs if there's no mist.'

Olivia moved on, followed by a preoccupied Raff. She gazed at the wooded slopes of the Surrey countryside and remembered Mr Faber's reference to the South Downs. It was her own home landscape and was largely dominated by rolling hills and as the sun descended, shadowed valleys. She was swept by a feeling of homesickness, a longing for familiar sights and faces which welcomed her with smiles and trust.

Raff's impatient nose came prodding at her motionless feet. She turned and strolled towards the beautiful Georgian residence that was her husband's home. It was still impossible for her to regard it as hers, too.

Olivia wandered all over the house looking for Macaire. In the end, she asked Mrs Faber who told her that he had gone for a walk. The situation was so familiar, Olivia smiled to herself. Not round the estate, the housekeeper said. Probably to Box Hill, which was where he took all his problems. Although, she said, laughing, what problems a young man could have with a lovely young bride searching for him . . .

Macaire's out, Olivia thought. There's a telephone in the guest bedroom where we slept last night . . . It did not take long for her to be connected to Daniel Watling's home.

'Hallo, dear,' said Mrs Watling. 'How nice to hear from you. Enjoying your holiday? How far have you got? Oh, here's Daniel now.'

'Olivia?' The voice was restrained yet eager, which was typical of the speaker's personality. Olivia visualised Daniel's round face, with its honest eyes and sandy eyebrows echoing the colour of his hair. 'How's the weather where you are—cold, like we warned you? How's the car going?'

Olivia laughed. 'What a lot of questions, Daniel! But it's so nice to hear familiar voices.'

'Is there something wrong?' Daniel asked. 'Are you sorry you went?'

'Oh, Daniel, so much has happened since I left home I can hardly begin to tell you.' There was a scuffle at the door and Raff, surprisingly, flung himself at Olivia's legs. Since Macaire had told her that the dog was not usually allowed upstairs, she assumed he must be following Mrs Faber around. 'First, though, how's the house? You're keeping an eye on it? It's very kind of you. Anyway, how are you?'

'All the happier for hearing your voice.'

Olivia absently fondled Raff's ears as he sat patiently beside her. 'Daniel, there's something I must tell you. It might come as a shock. I'm—I'm married.' There was a long silence. 'Daniel,' Olivia said anxiously, 'are you there?' There was a faint reply. 'I'm sorry, Daniel, but it—well, just happened. I can't explain on the phone. It's very complicated, and you'll hardly believe it when I tell you. I—I know you—well, you liked me and hoped one day I'd change my mind and——'

'It's all right, Olivia,' Daniel answered resignedly. 'I know you turned me down, but I didn't quite give up hope. But,' he sighed, 'I do understand. When are you coming—— Sorry, I suppose this isn't really your home now, is it? Where does your——' Olivia heard a large swallow, 'husband live?'

'In Surrey, not far from Dorking. It's a beautiful house. Daniel, I wish you could see it . . .'

'Are you happy?' Something in her tone must have reached him.

She had to speak carefully. 'As happy as the circumstances allow.' Raff flopped down, nose on paws. 'I'm surprised you didn't read about it in the papers.'

'Oh?' Daniel sounded puzzled. 'I've been so busy the last week or two I haven't read more than the headlines, and my mother never reads any newspaper if she can help it, as you know.'

'I must go. I'll contact you again soon. 'Bye, Daniel.'

Olivia rang off and stared through the window at the extensive estate which surrounded the house. Then she sighed deeply and half-turned—to see her husband leaning indolently against the doorway.

'So that was the man who didn't get the girl?' His arms were folded and Olivia noticed with a skip of the heart how the exercises must have greatly improved his injured arm. His waist was spanned by a leather belt. His pants were worn thin at the knees and his shirt was open at the neck. His eyes were cool, his expression hard. The implacable man at the farmhouse door was back again . . . 'Were you hankering after him so much,' he continued, 'that you couldn't wait to hear the sound of his voice?'

Raff had risen and gone to lie at his master's feet. Now Olivia knew how the dog had come to the guest room—at his master's side. Which meant that Macaire must have listened to most of her conversation.

'If I'd known you were in the habit of eavesdropping,' she counter-attacked, 'I'd have closed the door.'

'And I would have opened it. I came to find you to tell you I've instructed Mrs Faber to move our belongings to my suite of rooms. Having found you, I waited patiently until your phone call ended. So "eavesdropping" was hardly the right word, since it implies that what you were saying was secret and was something you didn't want me to hear. Is that true?'

Olivia tried desperately to remember what she had said to Daniel. 'I had nothing secret to say to him. You must have heard me tell him I was married.'

'And falling over yourself to apologise for the fact. Not to mention implying that, if you could, you'd tear yourself in half and give part to me and part to your boy-friend.'

'Boy-friend? He's not that, Macaire.'

He said to the dog, 'Out, hound. Kitchen,' and closed the door on the reluctant animal. He turned the key and Olivia gripped the seat of the chair she occupied. 'We're being strictly formal nowadays, are we?' he commented. 'At the farmhouse I was Mac. Why not Mac now?'

He strolled towards her, eyeing the revealingly tight

tee-shirt which she wore with her slacks. His right hand caught her wrist and tugged her upright to face him. Her head tipped back, her blood flowed faster. 'So you're not happy?'

She started to protest, but he cut in, 'What's wrong? Annoyed that all I did last night was hold you in my arms? Would you have been happier if I'd made love to you? Like this——' He pushed her down on to his bed and went with her. 'And this.' His hand found the bare midriff and pushed upwards under the shirt, seeking the warmth and shapeliness of her femininity.

'Please, Mac,' she pleaded, 'not now. Someone might come in——'

'I've locked the door.'

'Someone might call you. Your manager——'

'Right now he can go to hell.' He became irritated by the barriers separating them, pulled her to her feet and tugged the tee-shirt over her head. Soon he was satisfied and pushed her down again, their bodies touching and clinging and bringing a searing desire to life.

His head lifted and his hand clamped round her chin, holding her face so tightly she could not look away. His eyes were brilliant as they delved into hers, probing into the very essence of her. It was, she thought bemusedly, as though she were a piece of music and he were analysing each note of her, the better to interpret and play her, thus increasing the pleasure she gained in joining as one with him.

Then his hands—both of them, she noticed abstractedly —trailed her body, lightly stroking, skimming her thighs, her hips, her waist, and finally, bringing radiance to her flushed cheeks and dazzled eyes by claiming indisputable possession of her swelling breasts.

His lips roamed, upwards to her throat, her chin and finally her mouth, teasing every part of her lips until they responded with abandon.

There was a knock on the door, but they were too far gone into their private world to care. Eventually the caller went away and Olivia's arms wound more tightly around her husband's neck, holding him even closer. In her desire to yield herself to him without restraint, she urged herself against him until, supremely, ecstatically, she was possessed by him. And then the joy intensified.

It was some time later that they roused themselves. Raff's bark outside the window, Mr Faber reprimanding him, the spring song of the birds calling one to the other, all combined to remind them that another world than theirs existed and exerted its demands.

Macaire moved away and put an arm across his forehead. 'Well,' he said at length, 'are you still only as happy "as circumstances will allow"? Or have I shown you a glimpse of heaven? Do I rate higher in my lovemaking than your boy-friend would, if you had allowed him the intimacies you've allowed me?'

His harsh tone was like a heavy boulder crashing into the pool of contentment in which she floated. After the ecstasy they had shared, the hurt his words inflicted was almost unbearable. 'I really don't know,' she lashed out with the intention of giving pain for pain. 'The next time I see Daniel I'll have to ask him to make love to me so that I can make a comparison and report back to you.'

He turned on his side, grasping her throat. 'Why, you little——!'

The knock came again. 'Mr Delaney, sir, Mr Delaney!' Mrs Faber called. Macaire released Olivia and shouted in reply. 'There's someone to see you. It's Miss Brambella and she says she won't leave this house until she's spoken to you. And Mr Delaney, I think she really means it.'

CHAPTER SEVEN

'YOU'RE coming with me.'

'Mac, I can't.'

They faced each other across the bed. They had pulled on their clothes, but Macaire's shirt was only partially buttoned. Olivia had run a comb through her hair. Macaire had run a hand over his.

'I insist. You're going to meet Annetta. More important, she's going to meet you—and realise she's lost the game.'

He went round the bed and put his arm round her shoulders, propelling her towards the door. They walked along the landing and down the stairs. With his foot, Macaire pushed open the heavy oak door of the main reception room.

Macaire halted Olivia in the doorway. They were, to an onlooker, deeply in love. To an eye as discerning as that of the woman visitor, they had very recently consummated that love. Macaire looked down at his wife, then he turned her so that her mouth was uplifted to his. Their lips met, lingered and parted.

Why, Olivia thought in anguish, is he doing this? To provoke his former fiancée to jealousy? Which could only mean he still cared for her . . .

Macaire put his wife from him and, remaining where he was, smiled at his guest. 'Forgive me, Annetta. I couldn't resist responding to the love in my wife's eyes.' His own eyes hardened maliciously. 'Do you approve of my choice? She's all I could wish for. She's as unlike you as a wild rose from a plastic flower.'

'You fool.' The words came from someone who stood partly hidden by the opened door. 'You blind, crazy fool!'

Macaire pulled Olivia into the room. 'Well, well, my publicity manager. Ill-met, my friend. I should have known that wherever Annetta Brambella the great opera singer

118

goes, Fulton Hallinger couldn't be far behind. She is, after all, part of my publicity schedule, and I part of hers. Alas for you, Fulton, you're too late. I've got myself a partner. And, moreover, till death us do part.'

'You think so?' Annetta spoke in delicately accented English. 'You think wrong, Macaire.'

Olivia's eyes widened as she studied the famous star. Annetta Brambella was slender, black-haired and magnificently beautiful. Her hair was drawn back to reveal the perfect oval of her face. Her eyes were compelling and dark. Her dress of brown lace rose high to encircle her long neck. Gold earrings dangled, matching the gold pendant rising and falling on her breast.

As she looked at her host and hostess, her full lips formed a bitter curve. Her eyes fastened on to Macaire's and slowly she smiled. He did not respond. She murmured his name, but he stayed silent. A hand lifted towards him in an appealing, theatrical gesture, but he was unmoved. All of her tricks had failed. She looked quickly at Fulton who, with a nod, encouraged her to continue.

Viciously Annetta turned her attention to the girl at Macaire's side. By her expression of distaste with which she regarded Olivia's slim, carelessly clothed form, it seemed that the opera star held nothing but contempt for her former fiancé's bride.

She said spitefully, 'You've married this—this creature, when you could have had me back? I could hardly believe Fulton when he told me what you'd done. If you had wanted a woman for *that* purpose—and,' with a triumphant glance at Olivia, 'I personally know your intimate needs, don't I, darling?—heaven knows, such women are easy enough to come by these days, without making the liaison legal. A man with your sophisticated tastes married to a—to a——' she choked back a more insulting word, 'her!' she finished.

Sophisticated tastes? Olivia stirred restlessly against Macaire's side, but his arm, which was round her, pulled her closer. How little she knew of this man she had married so impetuously! Could she ever hope to live up to him, either in his intimate life, or his very public one?

Annetta, who had been watching the play of doubt over Olivia's face, smiled maliciously. She looked at Macaire. 'I wish to speak with you.' She glanced coldly at Olivia. 'Alone.'

Macaire made no move to release his wife but looked instead at Fulton. 'You heard what the lady said.'

Fulton smirked and covered his ears. 'I've suddenly turned deaf.'

Annetta looked pointedly at Olivia.

Macaire said, releasing Olivia, 'What you want to say to me can be said within my wife's hearing.'

Annetta glanced at the publicity manager as if for guidance. Again Fulton nodded, this time with greater emphasis.

Annetta's eyes flashed at Macaire. 'As you wish, but you will regret it.' Macaire lifted his shoulders. Annetta took a few paces towards him. It was almost as if she were on stage. 'I love you, darling,' she said softly. 'I have never ceased to regret the day I ran from you.' Macaire slipped his right hand into his pocket. 'I have never stopped loving you, not all the time I endured my marriage.'

'You're breaking my heart.'

Olivia watched unbelieving as Annetta's lips tightened to reveal her small white teeth. She had seen Raff bare his teeth in anger, but never before had she seen a woman do so.

'I want you to come back to me, Macaire. I want you to divorce your wife and marry me.'

'My God,' Macaire drawled, 'Fulton has rehearsed you well.' To Fulton, 'I congratulate you. She's a puppet on your strings. She performs the routine admirably. Annetta, you're wasting your time. I married the woman of my choice and I have no intention of letting that woman go.'

'You said at the time of the accident,' Annetta stormed, 'that you would never marry. Fulton was there. He heard you.'

'You also said,' Fulton Hallinger broke in, 'you would never trust a woman for the rest of your life.'

'So I changed my mind,' Macaire drawled. 'I also said—

and you were there to hear me—that I would never play again.'

Fulton looked disconcerted. Macaire smiled and murmured, 'That hit you where it hurt.'

Annetta continued, coaxing now, 'I want you to change your mind about that, too, darling. I want you to resume your career after treatment to your arm.'

Macaire taunted, 'How much is Fulton paying you for saying this?'

'You're playing a losing game, my friend,' said Fulton. His eyes, full of malice, went to Olivia. 'There's more to come.'

Annetta clenched her fists, but the actress in her summoned a glittering smile. 'I have it in my power, Macaire, to ruin you. I could degrade you in public. I could halt the sales of your recordings.'

'You intrigue me. How would you go about this terrible deed?'

Olivia felt her palms grow moist, her throat become dry.

Annetta smiled over-sweetly. 'Before you appeared downstairs just now, we talked to your housekeeper. She was a little indiscreet, although she regarded it as a joke. She told us a few very interesting things.'

'I can't stand the suspense,' Macaire responded.

Olivia felt her heart begin to pound.

Annetta continued, 'She told us that when you were in hiding, you went about in rags. You grew a beard. You were unrecognisable. You posed as a murderer. You pretended to be a rapist. And who knows,' with a contemptuous smile at Olivia, 'perhaps you were one.'

'Hence the precipitate marriage?' Macaire said coldly.

'Maybe.'

Macaire laughed harshly. 'Which makes me one of nature's gentlemen! Come, Annette, you of all people know me better than that.'

Olivia's breathing became deeper and faster. Her toes curled, her nails bit into her palms.

Fulton broke in, 'Your housekeeper also told us that you

turned away the girl—that girl—who asked you for shelter from the terrible weather. You turned her away not just once but twice. And even then she still came crawling back to you.'

He withdrew a cigar from his pocket and put a lighter to it. 'Think well, my friend, before you decide to stay faithful to the young stranger you married. All the ammunition with which your housekeeper unwittingly supplied us would, if placed in the hands of some unscrupulous journalist, be devastatingly damaging to your image.'

'You really think I care? In any case, it would be forgotten in a couple of weeks.'

'Not if we keep fanning the flames,' said Fulton. 'Mud such as that, once thrown, tends to stick. Your public, especially the women, would remember it every time your name was mentioned, or your picture was printed in the papers. No matter how brilliant your piano playing, it would be just that little bit tarnished by the memory of the demoralising things that happened to you when you were no longer in the public eye.'

'And how would all this benefit you?' Macaire asked, plainly unmoved. 'You'd be killing the goose that laid the golden egg—myself.'

'Ah,' Fulton replied, glancing again at Olivia, 'but I don't think I shall need to use such a weapon. You see, I think you'll see sense and not give me cause to apply such tactics to get you to return to the fold—unencumbered by a woman, however legal your liaison with her may be.'

'What is it they say?' drawled Annetta, with an exultant smile. 'Sow a little seed of doubt ... It would be enough to damage your image, Macaire. It would make people think and wonder—and hesitate before going to your concerts, pause before buying your records and cassettes.'

'What you're saying is the height of absurdity,' Macaire interrupted. 'You're also resorting to moral blackmail.'

'It does not worry me,' Annetta declared passionately. 'I want you back. I repeat that I would do *anything* to get you back, my darling.' Her eyes blazed into his. 'Anything, Macaire ...' Then they blazed, in a different way, into

Olivia's eyes. 'You understand, Mrs Delaney, that both Fulton and I share a determination to eliminate you from Macaire's life? And that we will win?'

Get rid of her, Fulton Hallinger had urged Macaire on the phone, *get her out of your life!* Olivia looked from one to the other.

'All right,' she shrieked, 'you've won the fight. If Macaire wants you,' to Annetta, 'he can have you. Although how he could love a scheming, unscrupulous, unprincipled she-devil like you, I simply cannot see.' There was no anger on the other woman's face, only insolence and triumph.

'Who said I loved her?'

Macaire's unemotional voice brought Olivia to face him. 'Who else is it you love,' she cried, 'if not your ex-fiancée? If you'd loved me, you would have told me so when I asked you. All you did was quote a poem at me. *'Love that never told can be ...'* Of course it couldn't because it wasn't there! So you can have Annetta Brambella, she's yours. Didn't you hear her tell you? Forget me. Tear up that marriage certificate. Divorce me, when the time comes.'

Tears threatened, but with iron determination she kept them at bay. 'I'm getting myself out of your life. Which is exactly what they want and no doubt, deep down, what you want. I'll go to Daniel Watling. He's solid and dependable and *loves me*. He'll not turn me away!'

How she reached the door Olivia never knew. She raced up the stairs, grabbed a coat from the wardrobe, her handbag from the floor and picked up a suitcase which had not yet been unpacked. The rest would have to remain.

Before she could change her mind, she hurried down the stairs—to find Macaire in the hall. He reached out and gripped her arm, but playing for the first time on the fact that his other arm was by no means fully functional, she twisted from him.

'You've got the woman you want,' she stormed. 'Let her fulfil all your sensual desires. She's familiar—and I mean familiar—with your manly needs. She left no one in any doubt about that.' At the door she put down her case and fumbled with the catch, unfastening it. 'Goodbye, Macaire.'

To her horror her voice wavered as she added, 'Good luck with'—she took a breath—'your career. And t-take heart, three years' separation will free you from our m-marriage vows.'

Her car was still parked in front of the house. She unlocked it and threw her belongings on to the back seat. She drove fast along the drive and braked sharply when she met the main road. In the few moments in which she had to wait for a break in the traffic, she took deep breaths to calm herself. She knew that if she did not, she would never reach her destination.

Driving through the traffic, Olivia had no time to dwell on what she had done. But once she found herself in open country, the tension inside her cried out to be released. She sought for a parking bay and found one which was empty. She drove into it and, when the engine was silent, she clutched at the steering wheel, letting her head fall forward to rest on her hands.

It was late afternoon when Olivia arrived at her home. She had eaten her second meal of the day at a restaurant, but the food, although well cooked, had slid almost untasted down her throat.

It was strange to be home. She had been away for barely two weeks, but if someone had told her she was mistaken and that it had really been two years, she would have believed them rather than the calendar.

The short straight driveway led to an old red brick house. Her Aunt Molly had not lacked for money. The good state of the building informed a visitor of this, even before they saw the solidly-constructed wooden furniture and good quality carpets and curtains.

When Aunt Molly had died and the lawyer had told Olivia that the house and its contents now belonged to her, she had been dazed. When he had added that her aunt's money also had been left to the girl who had cared for her so painstakingly for ten years, Olivia had stared in disbelief.

As she let herself into the house, she thought yet again,

All this can't be mine! She climbed the stairs to her room, carrying her case. The first thing that greeted her as she opened her bedroom door was the larger-than-life poster portrait of Macaire Connal. It showed him seated at a piano, one hand in contact with the keys, the other poised above them. The lighting had been so cleverly devised by the photographer that it shed a golden glow on to the subject of the picture, giving him an intriguing mysticism which tantalised and played havoc with feminine emotions.

As she studied the total absorption of Macaire's face, she had to concede that, intimate though she had been with him and although she wore his rings, her knowledge of him only skimmed the surface of his personality. In the tempestuous ten days or so of their marriage, she had learned that that mysticism in his character which the photographer had caught did in fact exist. It was really no clever creation on his part. Macaire Connal *was* enigmatic, inscrutable and, in essence, unknowable.

Olivia found her hand reaching out to trace the thick black eyebrows, touch the dark hair, the straight nose, the full, sensual lips. Her finger moved around his jawline and over the provoking chin. She gazed into the intense, unfathomable eyes and wanted to cry out because he did not respond.

It was as though he was with her, alive and vital and powerfully masculine. Her hand groped again, craving to make contact, only to find the empty air and a heartbreaking nothingness.

It was like a terrible dream. Why didn't he look at her, smile, take her in his arms ... She checked her thoughts abruptly, covering her eyes. This was bordering on hysteria. She must accept the fact that they might never meet again. Those threats which Annetta and Fulton had made were real and she had no doubt that, if necessary, they would act upon them.

She had run from her love, *for* her love. It had been for his sake and his alone.

Mrs Watling opened the door to Olivia. 'Delighted to see

you, dear,' she said. 'Although I must admit I'm surprised. In the circumstances, we hadn't expected you back for weeks.'

Olivia supposed she was referring to her marriage. Mrs Watling was tall, well-dressed, well-built and dominating. Since she was a widow and had had only one child, her son was all she had left to dominate, and dominate him she did!

Daniel had not, Olivia had observed with amusement, made much of an effort to escape from his mother's subtle but resolute clutches.

'I thought,' Mrs Watling went on, 'that you'd be enjoying a blissful honeymoon.'

Daniel came in, held Olivia's hand a little longer than his mother approved of and smiled a little dispiritedly. 'You let me down,' his look said. He had not dared to say the words aloud. He had probably never told his mother that once he had asked Olivia to marry him.

'What are you doing here?' he asked. 'Is your—husband with you?' Clearly the word was distasteful.

'No. I—I had to come home to attend to—well, things.'

He frowned. 'On your honeymoon? Who was it you married, anyway? I wasn't aware that you knew anyone, any man, well enough to——'

'It was all very sudden. I——' she looked at Mrs Watling. Why should she feel so guilty, when she had done nothing wrong in marrying the man with whom she had so swiftly and apparently so disastrously fallen in love? 'It's difficult to explain,' she went on lamely. 'I knew him—yet didn't know him. It sounds silly but—it's someone you might have heard of. You know Macaire Connal?'

Daniel and his mother looked at each other. 'Not,' Daniel said, eyes wide with shock, 'the concert pianist? You can't mean him?' Olivia nodded. 'But wasn't he involved in some kind of scandal——'

'An accident,' his mother broke in with a touch of gloating, 'as a result of drunkenness after his fiancée ran away before their m——'

'I know all about that,' said Olivia, hoping her cool

dignity would hide the turmoil inside her. 'And it wasn't drunkenness that caused the accident, whatever the newspapers said at the time.'

'Well,' Daniel commented, 'he injured his arm among other things, which meant he could never play——'

'Oh, but he will play again.' She remembered what Macaire had told her at the farm. 'He's—he's going away for a while to have treatment on his arm, and then put in an intense period of practice to get back into top form. That's why I've come back. I'll be staying for—well, some time.'

'Surely,' Mrs Watling persisted, 'he has a home of his own? Couldn't you have lived there?'

Olivia feigned a shrug. 'I thought it a good opportunity to tidy up my own affairs.'

To her relief, they accepted the explanation. Mrs Watling said with a smile, 'I don't know how you can bear to be parted from your bridegroom at this stage of your marriage.'

Olivia smiled and said to Daniel, 'I hope you've been using your own particular room in my aunt's—in my—house while I've been away?'

'The one he uses as a dark room?' Mrs Watling answered for her son. 'I've hardly seen the boy, he's spent so much time in there! Never mind, it keeps him occupied.' And, she was no doubt thinking, away from the opposite sex.

When Olivia returned home, Daniel went with her. He had, he said, been very disappointed to hear of her marriage. His tone was so much that of a sulky boy that Olivia answered sharply, 'But, Daniel, I've never encouraged you to think of me in any other way than as a friend.'

He walked with his head forward, staring at the footpath. 'I know you turned me down, but I didn't give up hope. You're not the sort to be happy in the sophisticated kind of world a man like Macaire Connal must live in.'

As they entered the house, Daniel asked, 'Was the reason you gave for coming back here true? That your husband was going away for treatment and work? Or did you discover your marriage wasn't working?'

Olivia hesitated for some time. 'Yes,' she said at last, 'it was true. But,' she sighed, 'there were other reasons. Please don't keep questioning me, Daniel. There are things——' her voice wavered. 'I just can't tell anyone. Not even you.'

Daniel lifted a shoulder. 'If that's how you want it . . .' He turned the handle of a door which opened off the entrance hall. Olivia's aunt, hoping as it happened in vain for a future marriage between her niece and her best friend's son, had for some years allowed Daniel to use the room for his photographic work. 'You don't mind if I see to some negatives?'

'Of course not. Just carry on as if I weren't here,' she said.

He needed no second invitation.

Some days passed, all of the same pattern. It was, however, disrupted one morning by a telephone call from London.

Hope had Olivia's heart thudding, but when the caller announced his identity, that hope died away like the final notes of a symphony.

'Harvey here,' the man said, 'Dick Harvey of International Press. Am I speaking to Mrs Macaire Connal?'

'You're speaking,' said Olivia, 'to Mrs Olivia Delaney.'

'Ah.' The journalist was not discouraged by her cool reception. In fact, he seemed pleased. 'Just the lady I'm looking for.'

'Do you mind telling me,' Olivia asked sharply, 'how you came to be in possession of my telephone number?'

'Does a lady by the name of Faber mean anything to you?'

'Yes, but——'

'Good. Now we're on the same wavelength. Er—Mrs Delaney, is there any truth in the rumour that your whirlwind marriage to Macaire Connal is breaking up?'

'None at all,' Olivia replied firmly, glad that she was, when necessary, able to put on a convincing performance. 'I can't think where you got the idea.'

'From a certain—er—lady who shall be nameless?'

A short silence, then Olivia answered, 'If you're referring

to a certain opera singer who is a colleague of my husband's——'

'His ex-fiancée, Mrs Delaney ...' The journalist's voice was silky.

'Remember the "ex", Mr—er—Harvey.' Had her tone been quelling enough?

It seemed that nothing would lessen this man's boldness. 'This—er—lady has told me unequivocally over the telephone that when the necessary time has elapsed, Mr Connal will be starting divorce proceedings against you for desertion.'

Olivia wanted to shout, 'Then tell that—er—lady that if she doesn't stop trying to tear my husband and myself apart——' Instead she remained silent.

'Mrs Delaney, are you there? Do you wish to make any comment on the lady's statement?'

'None, thank you.'

'Can you at least tell me where your husband is?'

So even the press didn't know where Macaire had gone? 'In the country. For treatment, recuperation and hard work.'

'Which is what Mrs Faber told us.' Which meant, Olivia concluded, that not even Macaire's housekeeper knew his whereabouts. 'In other words,' the man persisted, 'it's a close secret?'

'A very close secret,' Olivia echoed. 'Thank you for calling, Mr Harvey.' She rang off.

Olivia wandered to the living-room and sank into an armchair. It seemed that the leakage of poison, rumour and innuendo had begun. Annetta Brambella was keeping her word. If Olivia Delaney and Macaire Connal did not dance to her tune, it would not be long before hints of a scandal—the 'sowing of the seeds of doubt' which Annetta had hinted at—began to appear, tucked away in the corner of some newspaper. The trouble was that seeds had a habit of growing ...

Days passed, then merged into weeks during which Olivia had received neither letter nor phone call from Macaire. If Mrs Faber had been able to give her address to a newspaperman, surely Macaire must have been the one to discover it. He had probably found her other suitcase, opened it and discovered the address and telephone number on a label inside.

If he had been able to cut her out of his life with such ease, then his assertion that he had married her only because she was there must have been true. Macaire, however, was never out of her mind. When she went to bed, his absence was a torment, the shape and form of him an elusive glimpse of paradise out of reach.

March had long since become April and then it was May. The garden, which was large, claimed most of Olivia's attention. Daniel came and went in the house, using his key to let himself in and disappearing most times into his dark room. Now and then he would mow the lawn for Olivia, or spray the apple trees or repair a window catch.

One afternoon, weary of gardening and damp with perspiration from the sun's warmth, Olivia took a bath. Her aunt had determinedly refused to have a shower installed, a fact which Olivia now regretted. 'A quite unnecessary addition to a perfectly adequate bathroom,' her aunt had always said whenever Olivia had tentatively mentioned the idea. 'We have a perfectly good, functional bath.' And there the matter had always ended.

For some time Olivia lay soaking. The washing of her moist, pore-clogged skin was finished. Now there was time to relax, to forget for a while the unhappiness that haunted her, shrouding even moments of near-content with sadness.

At every opportunity she played Macaire's recordings, listening to his every note, appreciating the delicacy of his interpretation and perceiving every mood change. No wonder, she often thought, Fulton Hallinger did not want to let him go. No wonder the man wanted to ensure that such talent was retrieved and returned, with all its old brilliance, to the world of music.

She swished the water over her. But, she thought defiantly, in the achievement of that aim, why should I be cast out from Macaire's life like a piece of worn-out clothing? She would fight with every weapon—but how? With whom? With the only thing she had left of the man she had married—memories? She could not cling to the shadow of a phantom, which was what he had become to her in the past weeks, haunting her night and day.

There were two rings at the door, one short, one prolonged. It was probably Mrs Watling come to call Daniel from the darkroom. There were voices, and both were male. There was an exchange of words, and it did not sound friendly. The front door closed.

Footsteps mounted the stairs and Olivia grew frightened. The door was too far away to lock now. She never turned the key against Daniel because she knew he would never, under any circumstances whatsoever, enter any room in her house without invitation or permission.

He must, she reasoned, be coming to ask her something, talk through the door . . . It opened and she shrieked, 'No, Daniel, you can't——' Her heart almost stopped beating. The rest of the sentence came out in a dazed whisper, '—come in.'

'Thanks, sweetheart, for the invitation. But being your husband, I hardly needed it.'

'Macaire,' she choked, 'I didn't know——'

'Obviously,' was the clipped reply. 'It was Daniel you were expecting, wasn't it? He let me in. Now he's gone out Were you waiting for him to join you? Was the water cooling too rapidly for you both to enjoy yourselves?'

Olivia grabbed a face-cloth and spread it over her, using her hands to cover other parts. 'Will you get out?' she snapped between her teeth.

'Now, now, my love, is that the way to greet a husband you haven't seen for nearly two months? You ran out on me, remember?' He sat cornerwise on the side of the bath. 'And you didn't even say goodbye.'

He twitched the flannel from her breasts, reached down and fondled each one. She fought off his hands—then realised that his arm was now back to normal. With his wrists in her hands, which were passing their dampness on to the dark hairs they crushed, she said, 'Macaire, your arm—

it's better?' He nodded. 'Oh, Macaire!' Tears rushed into her eyes.

For a long moment he gazed into them. As the mist cleared she saw his face, the face which filled the poster on her bedroom wall and at which she had gazed every day of their separation. It was here now, near enough to touch. The mouth was smiling but with a hard, cynical contempt.

'You kept your word.' Olivia frowned at the statement. 'About going to your boy-friend. "He loves me," you said. Now you're sharing his house, no doubt the same bed. Strange,' he retrieved his hands and rubbed his cheek, pretending to be puzzled, 'how you let me break you in. Maybe the boy-friend was so inhibited he wasn't capable until another man——'

She rolled the face-cloth into a ball and flung it at him hard. It caught him on his neck and fell to the ground. He bent over her, gripped her under the armpits and hauled her to her feet. Water ran from her in rivulets. 'No, no!' she shrieked.

'Yes, yes,' he mocked, and scooped her bodily from the bath, holding her against him.

'I'll make your jacket wet,' she spluttered.

'It's waterproof. Now be still, my beauty, or you'll have my arm back to what it was.'

Fearful of inflicting further injury, with great reluctance she obeyed. She tugged a handful of his hair, crying, 'Put me down!' Her plea had no effect, so she said plaintively, 'I'm cold, Macaire. Please give me the towel.'

He smiled. 'I'm feasting my eyes, my love. Two months away from such beauty has sharpened my appetite.'

'You've had Annetta.'

'Have I?' The mocking amusement had left him. The coldness had returned. He lowered her to the floor and she dived for the bath towel, wrapping it round her, sarong-style.

'That's why I left you,' she said, her eyes blazing into his. 'To give you back the woman you really loved.'

'You're an incredible liar, my own.' His arms folded across his chest. He towered above her, making her feel insignificant. 'You left me to come here, to join the man *you* really loved.' He looked around. 'He might have had the bathroom modernised.'

'Macaire,' she whispered, 'you're wrong. This is *my* house, not Daniel's.'

He frowned. 'You're lying again.'

She shook her head furious. 'It's mine, left to me by my aunt.'

The change in his face frightened her. Here was the man in the farmhouse again, ruthless, frightening, capable of anything . . .

'So what's he doing here? Sharing your house instead?'

'No! He's keen on photography. There's a room down-stairs which my aunt allowed him to use as a darkroom. He still uses it.'

'As good an explanation for a man's presence in a house as any I've heard.'

'You don't believe me?'

'I told you, you're a liar. You've lied in other ways. About having no boy-friend when I questioned you before we married. And about this house.'

'I didn't lie about the house, Mac.' A flicker passed across his eyes at her use of the abbreviation of his name. 'I just didn't tell you—everything about myself.'

'You let me think you were poor.'

'You never asked about my financial status.'

'After we were married, there were plenty of opportunities for you to tell me.'

This was so true, Olivia coloured. She recalled her decision to keep him in ignorance of her inheritance in case the knowledge of it might change the situation between them. She wrapped the towel more tightly around her and sought his eyes. 'Would it have made you decide against marrying me if I'd told you?'

His eyes skimmed over her smooth shoulders. 'My attitude towards you might have been—different.' He reached out and removed her bath cap, watching her hair fall to cover her shoulders. 'No wonder,' he remarked, his eyes narrow, 'you stayed so faithfully at your aunt's side all those years. Knowing that all this would be coming your way——'

'I did *not* know. I assumed my aunt was leaving everything to charity.' His expression was sceptical. 'It's true, I tell you!'

His fists went to his hips and he looked her over. 'Carry on, dry yourself.'

'I'm dry, thanks. Anyway, why did you come here?'

He lounged against the bathroom wall. 'I intended to ask you to come back with me.' Her heart leapt, her eyes brightened. 'But not now,' he said brutally. With a sadistic smile, he watched the eagerness die away. 'Not after being mistaken for "Daniel" who was told to "come in" to your bathroom and join you in the bath. And don't tell me you said, "No, Daniel, you can't," because that was simply coy provocation on your part. Anyway, the bathroom door wasn't locked.'

'Oh, I——' Explanations would be useless. 'You do think highly of me!' she stormed, adding the lie, 'I wouldn't come back with you now even if you asked me. Anyway,' she counter-attacked, 'you've got Annetta. You don't want me with you—except for the look of the thing.'

'The "look" of anything doesn't matter to me, my love. The little wife by a famous man's side is not regarded as good publicity by my manager. A little notoriety, even if invented, with another woman offstage—especially one who's famous in her own right—adds spice to a man's reputation. Makes the women think it could be them.'

'You're contemptible.' He gave a deep, mocking bow. She went on, 'So you don't want me around? As Fulton Hallinger says, it would spoil your image?'

'Even if I didn't want you around, why should you worry? You've got your own man in your life, which is why you left me. He "loves you", remember? Your words, darling.'

In her agitation her hold on the towel loosened and part of it fell to one side. She groped for it—too late. He was gripping the towel and unwinding it, leaving her defenceless and vulnerable both to his eyes and his hands.'

'By heaven,' he muttered, 'it's time I reminded you whose

woman you really are.' He threw the towel aside, scooped her into his arms and carried her out of the bathroom. She kicked and struggled and he ordered, 'Stay still. You'll hurt my arm,' and at once she obeyed.

She continued the fight with her words. 'You can't—you mustn't—Why don't you go away? Leave me alone, Macaire. Go to Annetta for love as you used to do. She's more to your taste than I am. She said so . . .'

'Quiet, woman! Which room?' He caught sight of the poster of himself on the wall and swung her into her bedroom. 'Ah, I've seen it at last, that picture of me in front of which you bow down and worship every night. Your idol, who in a few moments,' his gaze raked her body indolently from head to toe, 'is going to ravish you and make you his so completely that every single thought you have of your boy-friend will go out of your beautiful head.'

He dropped her on to the bedclothes. 'How convenient,' he drawled, pulling free of his jacket, 'that you sleep in a double bed.'

'Macaire,' she made one last plea, feeling for the bed cover and wrapping it round her, 'please don't.'

He tugged at his tie, unbuttoned his shirt and threw it off. 'You didn't say that, sweetheart, on our wedding night.' There was no tenderness in his tone. He stood before her at last tall, male from head to foot, his shoulders even broader with the exercises he had undertaken, his waist and stomach lean and tight-muscled.

He threw himself beside her, pushed aside the bed cover and let his eyes devour every single enticing curve of her. He stroked, he caressed, slowly, slowly arousing her desires. His lips touched down and skimmed where his hands had been, until every part of her body was tingling with delight and anticipation.

He pulled her against him and his arms, hands and lips hardened with his own demands and needs. Now she knew that his desire equalled hers and she rejoiced, crying out with joy when his mouth moved from her throat to her breasts, urging closer to him and calling out his name.

Moments later ecstasy enveloped her and she belonged

once more totally and unreservedly to the man she loved.

They must have slept, but not for long. When Olivia stirred to wakefulness she found the bed cover over her.

Macaire still lay beside her. He was awake, but his arm was raised to rest across his eyes. Olivia moved and in their newly-discovered intimacy, was bold enough to wriggle across to his side and curl across him. He did not move. She walked her fingers through the dark hair on his chest, followed the line of his jaw, and playfully outlined his lips.

Taking courage from the fact that he did not repel her, she moved his arm higher to rest on his forehead, only to find that his eyes were closed.

'Macaire?'

'Yes?'

'You look pale.'

'I've been working hard.'

'And,' she tugged at his chest hair, 'playing hard?'

He lifted his head and gave her a quelling look. She smiled impishly up at him. He did not smile back. 'Annetta's lucky to have you all the time, Mac.' She rubbed her cheek against his arm. He shifted it irritably.

'What's the matter, Mac?' Her heart beat dully. 'We've just shared something precious——'

He pushed her aside and swung his legs to the floor, beginning to dress.

'You're not only a liar, my sweet. You're a hypocrite.'

She cried out as if he had hit her, 'What do you mean?'

He buttoned his shirt and fastened the waistband of his pants. '*Precious*, you called it, when there's a man in your life who's willing to come at your call, even if it's in the afternoon?'

She sat up. 'Are you still referring to the bathroom, when you walked in and I thought——'

'It was "Daniel".' He played mockingly with the name. 'And were disappointed to discover it was only your husband. Yes, I am referring to that.' He eyed her. 'And if you don't clothe yourself soon, I'll come again at your call, right now.'

Olivia looked down at herself, saw what he was seeing and pulled the cover to her chin. She watched in disbelief as he made for the door. 'You're going, Mac?'

'Why,' he drawled, 'do you want me to stay? Haven't you had enough?'

'Mac,' as he turned the door handle, 'you're wrong, *wrong*, about me. There's no one else I love but you, no one.'

'You expect me to believe that,' he answered, 'when you kept from me the fact that you owned a house—and of considerable value, too. How much else are you keeping from me?'

She remembered the large sum of money in the bank and could not keep the fear from her eyes.

'Yes,' he said, 'I suspected there might be other guilty secrets you're harbouring.'

She shook her head. 'There's nothing "guilty" about them.' Realising he had no intention of relenting, of showing any clemency at all, she made a final plea, whispering, 'You're my life, Mac.'

'Tell that to the poster on the wall,' he replied brutally. 'He'll be as deaf to your lies as I am.' He began to close the door, opened it again and said, 'Better still, tell it to your boy-friend the next time he comes to your house—and your bed.'

Seconds later she was alone. A car started up outside. The tyres spurted on the gravel and the engine roared into the distance, leaving behind a crushing silence.

CHAPTER EIGHT

IT was when Olivia opened her morning newspaper two weeks later that she saw a photograph of Macaire. Beside him, arm linked in his, stood a smiling Annetta.

To the uninitiated, it looked as if a chance photographer had caught the couple strolling in a London park. To Olivia, who knew better, it was a cleverly-posed publicity photograph. Fulton Hallinger was beginning his campaign.

The caption ran, 'Whispers of romance? Macaire Connal and Annetta Brambella out walking . . . Divorce hinted at for celebrated pianist . . . Annetta Brambella almost free of former marriage partner . . . Miss Brambella said, "I'll never leave Macaire again . . ." '

A few moments later, she had called Daniel on the phone. 'Yes,' he confirmed, 'our paper has a picture, too. He's standing with her near the entrance to the Royal Festival Hall. It says, Lovers reunited. "I was foolish to leave him", said Miss Brambella. "When our divorces are through, we intend to marry".'

'Don't go on, Daniel,' said Olivia, hoping that her voice sounded normal.

'I don't understand,' Daniel said. 'If he's divorcing you, what was he doing here the day I let him in?'

Olivia was glad Daniel could not see her face. 'We—we talked things over.'

'I'm sorry your marriage didn't work out,' said Daniel. 'But that means you'll be free again, doesn't it?'

'Does it?' she said thickly, and rang off.

On impulse and before reason could tell her she was being a fool, she decided to go to London. The time had come to renew her acquaintance with Fulton Hallinger, the only person who was in a position to tell her where her husband was. She called Daniel to tell him of her intention, but he tried to dissuade her. 'He won't tell you. What's more, it will give him a weapon to use against you.

He'll play cat and mouse with you, just to tantalise ..'

Olivia ignored Daniel's warning.

Fulton's office was up a flight of dark stairs in a slightly dowdy street not far from Oxford Circus. The rooms which his agency occupied were, however, better than the visitor had been led by its outward appearance to expect. The premises had been tastefully carpeted and decorated. The office furniture had been designed in the modern idiom in man-made materials with chairs that curved and moulded themselves to the occupant and desks which gave the impression of stepping into the next century.

Olivia had no difficulty in obtaining an interview with Fulton. It was not until she saw his blandly smiling face that she realised why he had agreed so readily to see her. *He'll play cat and mouse with you,* Daniel had said. It seemed that for once Daniel's wisdom had outstripped her own.

Fulton stood, but with a slowness that insulted. He motioned his visitor to a low modern chair but she chose the conventional upright secretary's seat near the desk.

'And why,' he said, sinking down, 'have I been honoured with a visit from the sweet, luscious, but alas, expendable Mrs Delaney?'

'Not for the pleasure it gives me to see you again, Mr Hallinger.' He threw back his head and laughed. It was an unpleasant sound. 'I want to know where my husband is, and since you're the only person I can think of who is in possession of such information, I've been forced to call on you.'

He picked up a letter opener and ran his fingers up and down the blade. 'No can tell, Mrs Delaney,' he responded with a taunting smile. So far, Daniel had been right all the way . . .

'I want to contact him urgently, Mr Hallinger.'

He dropped the letter opener, and stared. 'My God, you aren't pregnant?'

If only she could say 'yes'—would that have proved to be the magic word which would give her access to her husband's hiding place? She was tempted to nod, to play with him as he was playing with her. But she heard Macaire's voice in her mind. *You're lying again* . . . And this time he would be right.

'I'm not pregnant, Mr Hallinger.'

The desk, lightly constructed as it was, almost vibrated with his sigh of relief.

'Then,' he said slowly, leaning back in his chair, 'I can think of no other reason why you should want to contact your husband.'

'If I say I want to see him,' Olivia said angrily, 'that, to me, is sufficient.'

He smiled at her anger and she reproached herself for her sign of weakness.

'He's a long way from here, my dear. Much, much too far for an innocent and unprotected young woman like you to venture.'

Olivia frowned. 'You mean he's abroad?'

'Look,' he was growing impatient, 'I'm saying nothing. I just don't want him upset. His arm's almost one hundred per cent recovered. His playing is damned near as perfect as it was before he injured himself. In no time at all, he'll be appearing in public again and only the severest critic will be able to hear the imperfections. Given just a bit longer, even those will have gone and he'll be back at the top where he was before and where he belongs. Now do you understand why I don't want you to see him?'

There was a short pause. 'No,' Olivia answered hoarsely.

He thumped the desk. 'I'll tell you this—I'm going to do everything in my power to break up your marriage, use every weapon fair or foul to achieve my aim. And I'll tell you something else. I've booked him concerts all over the country. Concerts abroad, too, Europe, the States, Australia —you name it, he's going there. His first since his accident is coming along soon in London. I've advertised it in the papers, and on the Underground. I don't want any clinging, adoring little wife clutching his arm and cluttering up his life. I want him free, like he was before. Understand?'

'Then,' Olivia returned acidly, 'you'd better prise Annetta Brambella from his life, hadn't you? She's famous, too. She demands attention. If you don't detach her from him, she'll steal the limelight every time, pushing herself in on his publicity act.'

'Don't teach me my job, you anonymous little upstart!' A door closed nearby, there were descending footsteps. A woman's voice rang with laugher. Fulton listened and a spiteful smile crept across his thin lips. 'Now I'll teach *you* something.' He motioned with his head towards the window. 'Come over here.' She followed. 'Look down there.'

Two figures emerged into the street. One was Annetta Brambella, groomed, slender and as elegantly dressed as ever; the other was the even taller figure of Macaire Connal. Olivia gasped and stared down at the dark head. He lifted his hand to hail a taxi. As they waited, a flash bulb went into action. A photographer in wait had taken a picture.

'You—you miserable liar!' Olivia turned on Fulton Hallinger. 'You despicable cheat. He was here all the time!'

'Thanks for showering me with compliments, dear. Yes, he was. But he gave explicit instructions when I called him on the internal phone and said you'd arrived that under no circumstances would he see you.'

'I don't believe you,' she cried. 'You're making it up.'

He glanced down. 'They're still waiting. I've half a mind to get him back to corroborate my story.'

Olivia rushed to the door, hearing Fulton lift the sash window and call out. He was warning Macaire! She raced down the stairs and flung herself outside, only to see her husband drive away, Annetta beside him, in the taxi he had called.

Disappointment and misery drained her face of colour. Tears welled up—and the flash bulb worked again. The photographer gave a deep, smiling bow and made a thumbs-up sign to Fulton, who still gazed out of the window.

So it had not been Macaire he had spoken to, it had been the photographer to whom he had given instructions to get a picture of Macaire Connal's wife watching her husband drive away with another woman. Daniel had been right. Fulton Hallinger had won.

An advertisement on the Underground had informed Olivia on her way home that the London concert at which Macaire Connal was to be the soloist was fixed for three weeks ahead.

Olivia told Daniel about it and he offered to take her. She accepted gladly. For some reason she felt the need for moral support, although she doubted if Daniel, with his self-effacing manner, would be able to give her much of that.

It was with a beating heart that Olivia, with Daniel beside her, found herself in the entrance lobby of the famous London concert hall. Under no circumstances did she want to be seen by Annetta or Fulton Hallinger, so she pulled Daniel by the hand, climbing the steps to their seats so quickly they were both out of breath.

Even if tension had not already tied her emotions into knots, there would have been a feeling of eager excitement engendered by the impressive surroundings and the subdued anticipation of the audience. Daniel had brought with him a box of chocolates which his mother had given them. It seemed that she considered this a necessary part of all concert and theatre-going.

Daniel opened the box with a crackle of paper, setting Olivia's nerve-endings, already agitated, jangling unbearably. She could not accept a chocolate when he pushed the box across to her. She gave it back, telling him to eat as many as he liked. This he proceeded to do, presumably not wishing to upset his mother. Olivia had not eaten since lunch, having been unable to face the thought of food, let alone consume any.

They had each bought a programme and she flicked through her copy, seeing nothing—until she started again at the beginning and found herself gazing into her husband's handsome, serious face. His deeply intelligent eyes seemed to be reproaching her, the set of his mouth unforgiving.

Yet there was a profound sensitivity about his full lips

and the curve of his chin which made her wonder if his callous treatment of her during their earliest encounters, his terrifying pretence of being a criminal in hiding, had been on her part a fabrication of her imagination.

Daniel nudged her and she jumped. The present, the surroundings, the chatter around her faded in like a new sequence of a television film and she remembered the reason for their presence in the vast auditorium.

'Anything wrong?' Daniel asked.

'N-no. Just dreaming.'

He looked at her but did not comment. For once, she was glad that Daniel's sensibilities, sometimes blunted, were this evening sharper than usual. She pretended to study the programme notes in excessive detail and Daniel followed her example.

The first item was an overture by Mendelssohn. When the applause died down, and the piano was moved into position, there was an unbearable pause. Olivia found herself holding her breath and clasping her hands together so tightly they must have been giving her pain—but she did not feel a thing.

As the conductor of the orchestra led on the soloist a tremendous burst of applause reverberated around the auditorium. This man, she told herself, maltreating her lower lip, was not her husband. He was a stranger, a smiling, composed, devastatingly attractive stranger. She had not really lain in his arms, wrapped about with the golden aftermath of lovemaking. He had not talked with her, walked with her, carried her triumphantly into her bedroom only a few weeks before and coaxed and caressed her into complete surrender.

Her eyes were brimming and she could scarcely see him bowing in acknowledgement of his rapturous welcome. There was only a blurred sight of him taking his seat at the piano and sitting, momentarily, head bowed, seeking serenity and concentration before the performance began.

In the few seconds before the music filled the hall, Olivia told herself, Everything that took place between myself and the man seated at that piano was a fantastic and wonderful dream and never, ever, must I try to persuade myself otherwise.

The music being performed was Mozart's Piano Concerto Number Twenty-one. Macaire's playing had plainly returned to its highest standards, as near to perfection as pianist, critic and audience could ever hope for. Olivia watched and worshipped, every part of her the ardent devotee of the world-famous performer who held his listeners spellbound.

When the famous second movement of the concerto began to weave its spell, and the melodious phrases flowed from his fingers, reaching the heart of every one of the people present, tears ran unheeded down Olivia's cheeks. Try as she might, she could not keep the memories of their short but tempestuous marriage at bay. Her love for him enveloped her like the mist that had first caused their paths to meet and she groped her way about in it, hopelessly lost.

The applause at the end was tumultuous. Time and again the soloist was called on to return. Macaire bowed deeply, smiling, lifting a hand in acknowledgment, bowing again. Olivia leaned forward in her seat, but she was so far away, his features remained blurred. All she could discern was that the smile which illuminated his face was one of rejoicing in his achievement, of relief at having attained his old playing form and gratification at having given so many people so much pleasure. Then he was gone.

It was the interval and Daniel looked uncertainly at his companion. 'Do you want to go outside? Find the bar ...?' he asked.

'Daniel,' her hand rested on his arm, 'I'm sorry, but I must see Macaire.'

'How do you intend to do that? They won't let you near him.'

'I'll do something. Use my name ...'

'They may have had orders——'

'To keep me out, you mean?' She compressed her lips. She had not thought of that. She would not put any trick past Fulton Hallinger. 'I'll have to take a risk.' Daniel eased his way along the row of seats, Olivia followed and in a few moments they found themselves in the entrance lobby.

Bewildered by the crush of people, Olivia looked around like a trapped animal. Everyone, everything, was contriving to keep her from going to Macaire. She saw a commissionaire in a peaked cap near the swing doors and made for him, Daniel trailing behind with her coat over his arm.

Olivia produced her sweetest smile. 'Please,' she pleaded, her grey-blue eyes large and luminous with emotion which still had not died away, 'could you direct me to the stage door?'

He began to shake his head. '*Please*,' she persisted. 'I must see my husband. There's—there's an urgent message I have to give him. It was telephoned through after he left home———'

'A member of the orchestra, madam?' She had at least caught the man's attention.

'The soloist,' she replied, half-apologetically.

The man's eyes widened. 'Oh, Mr Connal, you mean? Of course, madam, I'll certainly tell you.' He did so, pointing outside, and giving precise directions. 'It says "Private" on the door, but take no notice. That's to stop members of the public . . .' But Olivia had gone, calling out her grateful thanks, with Daniel only a few steps behind.

If it occurred to the doorman afterwards that it was strange how the wife of a man as well-known in musical circles as Macaire Connal did not know the way to the stage door of a concert hall as famous as the one in which he was that evening performing—and had done so many times in the past—then it was too late for him to do anything about it.

'Please come with me, Daniel,' Olivia begged, and pushed her way outside, gathering the skirt of her long dress and lifting it free of the ground.

Daniel followed close, going with her round the side of the building and pausing in front of the door marked 'Private'. Olivia took a breath and turned the handle. They entered, closing the door behind them. It was dark in the passage and a man emerged from a small office.

'Sorry, madam,' he said, 'sir,' to Daniel, 'public not allowed in here.'

'I'm—I'm not public,' said Olivia, summoning a smile to cover her nervousness. 'I'm Macaire Connal's wife. I have an urgent message. It was telephoned through after—after he left the house.'

The man looked doubtful. He frowned at Daniel as if trying to puzzle out who her escort might be, if her husband really was the man she had named. 'Please,' she said, her voice rising appealingly, 'it's urgent. Just a few words——'

After another moment's hesitation, the man lifted his shoulders as if the action exonerated him from any responsibility. 'All right, this way. Mrs Connal,' he added.

Olivia could hardly believe her good luck. It seemed that Fulton Hallinger had not given orders for her to be kept out, because it probably had not occurred to him that she would have the audacity to attempt to see Macaire on such an occasion.

'Only you, though.' To Daniel, 'Sorry, sir. You wait here.' Daniel, glad to comply, nodded eagerly.

It seemed a long walk through corridors illuminated with subdued lighting. Some doors were open, revealing small, cluttered rooms, others were closed. The door on which the man knocked was closed, too. It bore a large figure one.

He opened the door and said, 'Sorry to trouble you, Mr Connal. Are you alone?'

Olivia's heart was throbbing. The answer to the question must have been 'yes', because the man went on, 'Visitor for you. Lady says she's got an urgent message. Says she's your wife. I took her at her word and brought her here. Hope that's okay?' He opened the door wider, revealing Macaire's visitor. 'All right, sir?'

'Yes, Sandy, it's my wife. Thanks for bringing her.'

The man called Sandy motioned her in with a polite hand, and went away. Olivia was face to face with the star of the evening. He was her husband and she could not think of a word to say.

Macaire leant back against the make-up table, hands in pockets. The mirror behind him reflected the daunting breadth of his back, the perfection of the cut of his formal black suit, the thickness of his night-dark hair skimming the collar of his jacket.

His long legs were crossed at the ankles, the muscles of his thighs and the hardness of his hips revealed by the tautness of the material covering them. He was so overpoweringly masculine, so arrogantly good-looking, Olivia felt her senses jerk to total awareness with the restlessness of a patient thrashing about in the grip of a fever.

'So what's the urgent message?' There was no friendliness in his voice.

'Macaire, you gave a wonderful performance.' Why did she have to sound so breathless? 'If anything, you're even better than you were before you—stopped.'

He inclined his head slowly and with a touch of mockery. 'My first visitor since the performance ended—it's well-known that I like solitude after performing in order to unwind—and she turns out to be not only my most devoted fan, but also my most complimentary critic.' A hard glint lit his eyes. 'I repeat, what was the urgent message?'

'There wasn't one.'

'Another lie.'

'No.' She shook her head violently. 'Not a lie, really. I just had to see you. I used it to break through all the barriers.'

He strolled towards her, standing so near she had to tilt her head right back in order to see his face. Their bodies touched. 'Never let it be said that there's an insurmountable barrier between my wife and myself.'

His hands stayed in his pockets. Hers lifted to rest on his arms. 'The day you came to my house, you said you were going to ask me to go back with you. I want to, Mac.'

He looked down at her swelling breasts pressed so intimately against him. His eyes probed the deep neckline of her dress, revealing the inviting cleft. His hands came to life and gripped her hips, urging that part of her anatomy against him, too. Olivia pressed her teeth into her lower lip, trying to control the uprush of desire his manoeuvres were causing, the contact of his thighs against hers, the feel of his fingers pressing painfully into the layer of flesh which covered her hip bones.

Suddenly she was in his arms, being kissed so savagely that his mouth was pressing her farther and farther back. As his teeth ground against hers, she clung to his shoulders for support, clutched at the back of his head and felt her bones melting as her body yielded to the cruel passion which seemed to have him in its grip.

Then she was jerked upright and thrust away. 'Too bad for you, my sweet, that I don't need you any more.'

He might have rolled her down a mountainside and watched her disappear into a ravine.

There were voices in the corridor. Laughter echoed, footsteps sounded Macaire asked, 'Have you come alone?'

If she answered the question with the truth, it would immediately drive yet another wedge between them. She decided to compromise with a half-truth. 'I'm here alone.'

From the look in his eyes he seemed to have accepted the statement—until a feminine voice from the door said, 'She lies, Macaire. A man is waiting for her. He's red-haired, a Mr Watling. I have just been talking to him. There is no doubt that he accompanied her to the concert.' It seemed that Annetta had opened the door noise-lessly, but Macaire could not have missed the arrival. Had he tried to trick her into being indiscreet in front of a witness?

The look which Macaire turned on his wife made her shake. 'Will you leave my dressing-room?' he said with icy politeness.

'Mac, won't you listen?'

He said through his teeth, his eyes burning, 'Get out.' He moved towards her.

'Mac,' her voice rose hysterically, 'it's you I love. There's no one else. Don't judge me by your standards.' Her words made him even angrier. He gripped her shoulders, urging her backwards. 'I haven't got a secret lover, Mac.' She tripped, twisting her ankle, crying out. He stopped while she lifted it and rubbed it, gritting her teeth and letting the tears brim over.

'She's pretending, Macaire,' came Annetta's spiteful voice, 'to get your sympathy. Do not be fooled by her tactics.'

'You,' Olivia snapped at the other woman, 'keep out of this!' Carefully she lowered her foot to the floor. 'Mac, Daniel's just a friend . . .'

The mere mention of Daniel's name brought a return of the anger. 'If you refuse to leave,' he said, eyeing her with contempt, 'I'll contact the management and have you thrown out.'

Olivia limped to the door, then swung round. 'That would do your image good, my darling husband. The star performer has his wife ejected from the concert hall, then proceeds to make love to his mistress in his dressing-room.'

Macaire snapped, his jaw rigid, 'Why, you little——' His hand lifted and Olivia limped towards him. 'Go on, hit me. I challenge you to hit me.' His hand stayed where it was. 'I'll *make* you hit me, then I can broadcast it to the press.' She took a deep breath. 'I *hate* you, Macaire Delaney, with all the life in my body. *Now* hit me!' Her glittering eyes challenged.

His hand lowered slowly. He turned away. It was the sight of his rigid back, telling her of his implacability, that made Olivia admit that her gamble had not paid off. She moved into the corridor, turned and said,

'I leave you to the mercies of your woman, the one you really want. With her at your side, you have a future in front of you which will be devoid of warmth, of laughter, of deep, unselfish love, of—of children,' her voice sank to a whisper, 'of me.'

Daniel had waited uncomplainingly. The doorman seemed to have given him a chair.

Daniel rose and smiled, then saw her distress. 'Olivia,' he held out his hand, and because he was at that moment

like a rock in a stormy sea, her hand reached out to grip his
—and a camera flashed. A photographer had appeared from
the doorman's office, having apparently been instructed—
no doubt by Fulton Hallinger—to await the precise moment at which to take the picture. There was no doubt
that, from his point of view, that 'moment' could not have
told a more incriminating story.

Next morning, when she opened her morning newspaper,
Olivia saw how Fulton Hallinger had had his revenge. On
page four there were two photographs. One was of Macaire
and Annetta in the street outside Fulton Hallinger's London
office. Their arms were linked and they were laughing at
each other. It was the picture taken of them the day she
had visited Fulton's office, only to be told by him that Macaire was away.

Joined to that picture was the photograph of herself,
taken moments later, when she had watched them drive
away. It appeared, from the clever way the picture editor
had arranged the photographs, that she had been only a
few steps distant from where they were standing, her arm
outstretched towards them. There was not a taxi in sight.

The caption said, 'Macaire Connal gives all his attention
to his rediscovered and famous girl-friend and ignores his
wife's plea to take her back. Better luck next time, Mrs
Connal?'

The second picture was of Daniel and herself reaching
out for each other at the concert hall. The caption ran,
'Macaire Connal's cast-off wife seeks solace from the love
of her friend Mr Daniel Watling.'

Olivia's first instinct was to tear the newspaper to
shreds. This she resisted, realising how futile an act it would
be. The story—and pictures—were no doubt carried by almost every national daily. Her second instinct was to telephone Fulton Hallinger. This, too, she resisted. Whatever
she might say to him, he would merely laugh. Her tactics
had to be more subtle than that.

However, she felt she owed an apology to Daniel and
dialled his number. To her relief, he answered. 'Have you
seen—?' she began.

'Yes, it's in our paper, too. It was a dirty trick, Olivia.'
He sounded sulky. 'I know it wasn't really your fault——'

'I assure you, Daniel, if I could have prevented it, I
would. I'm sorry for involving you in my problems. I hope
you and your mother will believe me——'

'Mother's already complained. She rang the editor of the
paper.'

'You don't mean she actually got through to the editor?'

'Well, no, but someone fairly high up spoke to her. He
said he was very sorry, but it was too good a story to miss.
When she said it wasn't a "story", it was a lie from beginning to end, because her son—me, of course—wasn't involved in any way, except on a friendly basis, with Macaire
Connal's wife, the man said he understood her point of
view, but that gentlemanliness wasn't one of a journalist's
virtues—he'd be no good at his job if it was—and he
couldn't let all the other nationals carry the story without
using it himself, too. And that was that.'

Olivia apologised again and rang off, hoping desperately
that the editor did not decide to print a story to the effect
that the 'cast-off' Mrs Connal's 'friend' was suffering from
a mother-complex due to having a dominating maternal
parent who treated her son like a child and did his com-
plaining for him.

She trod the living-room carpet, trying desperately to
formulate a plan. Somehow she must have her revenge
against Fulton Hallinger's evil machinations.

When the phone rang, her heart leapt. Her first thought
was—Macaire. Her second was that it might be the press.
It was neither. It was Annetta Brambella and it was plain,
as she spoke, that having her revenge was foremost in *her*
mind and heart, too.

Having announced herself in silvery tones, Annetta went
on, 'Do you remember, Mrs Connal—although it is really
Delaney, is it not?—that day I met you when I came with
Fulton to Macaire's beautiful house which, as I need not
remind you, is partly mine?'

Olivia murmured a reply, becoming conscious of how dry
her throat had become.

'You might also remember that little—shall we say—warning we gave if Macaire refused to dance to our tune and—oh, this is so difficult to say—unencumber himself from the ties of your marriage. Also I said that I would do anything——'

'Even,' Olivia broke in furiously, 'resorting to blackmail?'

There was a short pause. 'Yes, on consideration,' Annetta continued, 'even resorting to blackmail, I would do anything to get Macaire back, to take him away from you. Well, Mrs Delaney,' her voice took on the quality of purest silk, 'the time has come to remind you of that warning. You see, I did not like, one little bit, your seeing Macaire after the concert last night.'

'That's too bad!' Olivia retorted. 'I have every right to see my husband——'

'Did you,' Annetta cut in smoothly, 'see the newspapers today? Did you enjoy the spectacle of yourself, there, in front of many hundreds of thousands of readers, pleading with your husband to remember your existence? Well, Mrs Delaney, there will be worse—*much* worse—to come if you ever try to see your husband again. Don't think that I won't know, because Fulton and I—we have our spies, and our photographers—everywhere. Especially wherever Macaire may be. So your visit to him, no matter where he is, will not go unnoticed.'

'You frighten me out of my skin,' Olivia said with a sarcasm she was far from feeling.

Annetta's suave approach seemed to have deserted her. Her pronunciation became more accented as her displeasure grew. 'I will tell to the press that story of your first meeting with Macaire,' she raged, 'how he threatened you, and raped you, and nearly murdered you. I will tell them how he forced you to marry him——'

Olivia felt herself growing warm as one threat piled on the other. Exactly how much power did this woman possess to wreck Macaire's career? 'If you tell the press those things,' Olivia responded, speaking with an emphasis which was entirely false, 'you'll be telling them a load of lies.'

'*Lies, lies?*' Annetta shrieked. 'I, the great Brambella, do not care. The press will believe whatever I tell them, do you hear? Do you want Macaire's name dragged through the mud? Do you want his future ruined just when he has fought his way back to the top? If you do not want all this, then keep away from him. Never, *never* see him again.'

Olivia was glad Annetta could not see the anxiety in her face. She said, feigning a hint of amusement, 'You'd do all that, Miss Brambella, when you profess to love Macaire?'

'I, love Macaire?' she cried, her silvery tones two or three octaves higher than normal. 'Have I ever said that I loved him? No, Mrs Delaney, it is that I *want* him—and there is a great difference. So why should I care about his career when I have a career which will be more than sufficient to provide for us both? Just as long as I have him . . . As long as I can take him from *you!*'

She rang off on a theatrically triumphant note.

Olivia put a shaking hand over her face. She was stunned that such a callous, self-seeking woman could have found her way to Macaire's heart, and there was surely no doubting that she had done so. If she had not, how was it that when, three days before their marriage Annetta had run away with another man, Macaire had gone to pieces—no matter how he had denied the accusation when she had made it at the farmhouse—sufficiently to have crashed his car?

With her fingertips pressed against her temples, she tried to reason out her own future. Some sixth sense told her that the parting of the ways had come. Her life, changed radically by her meeting with and marriage to Macaire, must from that day onwards change again.

The idea hit her as though it had spun out of the orbit of her subconscious mind like a meteorite hitting the earth. She would return to the farmhouse!

From that moment of realisation sprang a series of actions over which she seemed to have little control. They were being dictated to her like railway station announcements echoing phantom-like over passengers' heads.

The farmhouse must be made fully habitable. At this distance it would be difficult to contact a building contractor and an interior decorator. But by getting in touch with the reporter, Peter Ivens . . . That was the answer!

It was through directory enquiries that she discovered the telephone number of the *Moorland Evening Herald*. When the call was connected she was relieved to hear that Peter Ivens was at his desk and would speak to her at once.

'Hi, Mrs Delaney,' he said, 'nice to hear from you again. How are you keeping?'

No mention, Olivia thought, of her famous husband although, being a newspaper-man, he must, in the course of his work that morning, have looked through the national dailies. Having done so, he could not have failed to see the photographs.

Silently, she thanked Peter for his discretion. Aloud, she said, 'I'm going to ask a favour of you, Mr Ivens——'

'Pete's the name to my friends.'

'Well, Pete, then,' she said, laughing. 'I'd like to repay you for the favour I'm going to ask, but I don't . . .' Her voice trailed away. 'Just a moment,' she commented thoughtfully. 'Yes, I do!' She would play Fulton Hallinger and Annetta Brambella at their own game!

'Do what?' Pete asked.

'Know how to repay you for the favour. But that can wait. There's something I'd like to ask you to do for me.'

'Ask away, Mrs Macaire Connal Delaney.' She winced at the name, at the pain that came with it, the memories both sweet and bitter.

'Pete,' she said as lightly as she could manage, 'I've decided to get away from it all. I've made up my mind to go back and live in the farmhouse.' He did not answer. It was as though he was waiting, as if his reporter's nose scented a story. 'But Pete, please—this is all off the record. Promise?'

A short sigh, then, 'I promise. I take it you'll be returning—alone?'

'So you've seen the morning papers. I thought you might. Yes, alone. But as you probably know, the building's in a bad state of repair.'

'That's putting it mildly.'

'Yes, well, it's that that I'm asking your help about. You see, it needs a lot of work done on it to make it really habitable. I'm living so far away, I don't know whom to contact in the area and——'

'You'd like me to do that side of it for you? That's okay. I'll be delighted to help, considering your wedding gave me a story that put me on the journalistic map, as it were, not to mention increasing my bank balance by quite a bit. Yes,' he said, after a pause, 'I think I know the right building contractor for that kind of work. He might not be cheap, but he'd be fast, which I imagine is what you'd like in the —er—circumstances?'

'Yes, yes,' Olivia answered eagerly. 'And please don't worry about the cost. I have money, Pete. Not—not my husband's, it's my very own. You see, my aunt died——'

'And remembered you in her will,' he said, amused. 'I get it. Okay, so I'll——'

'And a decorator, Pete, it badly needs——'

'Redecorating? That's where my father would come in. You see, he's an interior decorator. He'd be delighted to oblige and at a moment's notice. He's semi-retired and getting restless. It would keep him occupied.'

'But that's wonderful, Pete! I want to move in quickly, you do understand?'

'Of course I do. Domestic pressures, demands of the public on a great artist . . .'

'If only that were all, Pete. Mac's publicity manager has vowed to break up our marriage.'

'He has? The louse!'

'Not only that. Annetta Brambella's threatened me—it's blackmail really. Unfortunately, she heard about how I came to meet and marry Mac and she says that if I don't stop seeing him, she'll give the press a twisted version of the circumstances of our meeting and sudden marriage and how he pretended to be a criminal and so on. She might even hint that he *is* one and that he's hiding some terrible crime.'

'I know. A smear campaign which isn't based on truth but innuendo. Could be just as damaging to his reputation as if it were really true.'

'That's exactly right! She's determined to get him away from me by any means, fair or foul.'

'Nice woman! If there's anything I can do——'

'There is,' Olivia assured him. 'This evening, when I ring you about the farmhouse, would you be prepared to take a few notes? I've a story to tell. You'll be the one to hear it first. Then you can do what you want with it.'

'You're handing me a hell of a lot of pocket money on a plate, madam,' Pete said lightly. 'Are you aware of that?'

'If so, I'm glad. But all I want is for my husband's reputation to remain untarnished.'

'Well, the story will sell all over the world, but one thing worries me. Shouldn't the man concerned have a say in its publication?'

'It's for his sake I want it published. This will be the truth, exactly as it happened. If you don't write the correct story, Mac's manager, assisted by that leech of a woman called Annetta Brambella, will write another kind of story —a pack of lies calculated to bring Mac's career to an end.'

'Okay, you know best. You can rely on me. And—don't let that heel of a publicity manager get under your skin!'

After making herself a cup of coffee, Olivia made her third call of the morning. It was taking a risk, she was aware of that, but it had to be done. She dialled Macaire's house—and caught her breath. The ringing had stopped, the receiver had been lifted ... 'Delaney speaking.' The voice was curt and irritable.

Why couldn't it have been Mrs Faber? Olivia's breath came quickly, her lips grew stiff. She forced herself to say, 'I should like to speak to your housekeeper.'

There was a biting silence. 'Would you now? What's wrong with speaking to me instead?'

Her heart began to hammer, as it did every time she saw him, talked to him, touched him. 'A great deal,' she hit back. 'I'd get a more sympathetic hearing from Mrs Faber, for a start.'

'Ah, would you, then?' He spoke as if addressing a distressed child. Then the brusqueness returned and he mocked, 'Has the boy-friend deserted you after today's *shocking*, *undignified* and *libellous* exposure of your love for each other?' It seemed as if Fulton Hallinger had told Macaire of Daniel's mother's protests to the press. 'Well, if it's sympathy for that that you're after, my *darling* wife, don't come to me!'

'I'm not coming to you,' she shouted, certain that he was in the point of ramming down the receiver. 'I'm coming to collect my belongings. I'm moving out of your house, Macaire. I'm——' He would never know the effort it cost her to continue. 'I'm making our separation official.'

'So Mr Daniel Watling is asserting his "right" at last, is he? Defying Mother? I didn't think he had it in him! He wants you to himself and has told you, leave your husband or else . . .'

'No!' she shrieked, using anger to cover her tears. 'It's *your* girl-friend who's asserting *her* right. She's waving those threats over my head. Either I never see you again, or——' Her voice wavered uncontrollably.

'So, instead of putting up a fight, you're leaving me, as instructed. I thought a woman in love with a man fought and scratched and clawed to keep him. Obviously your saying you loved me was yet another lie.'

'What's the good,' she choked, 'of loving you when you love another woman? Anyway, I said I wanted to speak to Mrs Faber——'

'You shall indeed speak to Mrs Faber, my darling. The sooner you remove your belongings and everything connected with you from my house the better. When you come, I won't be here. In a few minutes I'm going to London. To-morrow I leave for a concert tour—Amsterdam, Paris, Munich . . .'

She could not stop herself, she had to ask, even though she knew it would be telling him indirectly of the pain she would be experiencing at his distance from her, 'How—how long will you be away, Mac?'

A short pause, then, 'Long enough. Goodbye.' He added mockingly, 'Thanks for the memories. They were beautiful while they lasted.' His hand must have covered the mouthpiece because she heard a muffled, 'Mrs Faber, my wife wants a word . . .'

'Good morning, Mrs Delaney.'

Good heavens, Olivia thought, is it still morning? It was as if a lifetime had passed since she had opened her eyes to the daylight.

Olivia explained her intention of driving to Surrey just after lunch and collecting the items she had left behind after her precipitate dash from the house. The housekeeper assured her that she would be there to welcome her, and when Olivia arrived two or three hours later, she was.

So, also, was a boisterous black dog who, unlike his owner, was overjoyed to discover that she had not disappeared from his life never to return. He ignored completely Mrs Faber's calls to heel and flung himself with abandon at the newcomer. He yelped and leapt and barked. When Olivia crouched down and hugged him, resting her cheek momentarily against his clean, soft fur, he sat patiently, panting deeply, until she released him, then started welcoming her all over again.

They went into the house and he quietened, following her into the kitchen as she chatted to the housekeeper; up the stairs when she went into the guest bedroom where her clothes still hung, then sprawling on the carpet while she filled her suitcase. There was not, after all, much to pack, since she had originally taken only sufficient for a two- or three-week vacation.

Having completed her packing, she wandered for the last time around the house. There were a few rooms she had not seen. In one was the hi-fi system Macaire had told her about. It was, as he had claimed, of the highest quality. Olivia longed to play one of his recordings, sitting back and listening objectively as she used to do, enjoying the music for its own sake, and not because of the memories and emotions evoked by her intimate knowledge of the player.

In another part of the house she found the music room which she knew must exist somewhere in the building. The ceiling was high and white and possessed ornate and intricate carvings. The room was large, yet contained a minimum of furniture. The place was obviously regarded by Macaire as a workroom. Even the decorations, the armchair and the unit suite which ran along one wall were of a neutral colour which would not distract the dedicated and concentrating mind.

Most important of all was the shining grand piano, standing centrally. On a table and on the floor were music scores of concertos and sonatas, piled one on the other. Against a wall was a floor-to-ceiling bookcase, the books arranged drunkenly.

With reverence, Olivia backed to the door. It was as if the essence of the genius which inspired the piano playing of the man called Macaire Connal was everywhere in that room. The body and mind of the woman who loved him and for so short a time had become part of him was still haunted by the feeling of hero-worship for the man she had once regarded as her idol. Had he, she thought as she closed the door, fallen from his pedestal? No, she thought sadly. He was ironically more out of reach than ever.

When she went into the kitchen to say goodbye to Mrs Faber, there were tears in the housekeeper's eyes as well as her own. 'Is there nothing you can do, Mrs Delaney? You would have been so good for him. When I saw the young lady he brought home as his wife I thought, She's the one for him. But now, here you are, going off and away . . .'

For a moment Olivia could not speak, then she pressed the housekeeper's hand, swallowing the tears. 'Where's Raff, Mrs Faber? I thought I'd say goodbye to him, too.'

The housekeeper glanced round, shaking her head. 'Must have gone off to some corner of his own.'

Olivia sighed. 'Never mind. Maybe it's just as well. He wouldn't understand when I drove away and left him, would he?'

Mrs Faber saw her into the car. 'I've packed your things in the back,' she said. 'There wasn't much.'

Olivia thanked her and waved as she began to drive away—then, to her astonishment, heard a muted whine behind her. She braked sharply, turned, reached down and moved a rug aside. Lying full-length beneath it, and looking very sorry for himself, was Raff.

'Oh, no!' Olivia exclaimed. 'Not you. How did you— Mrs Faber,' she wound down the window as the house-keeper came hurrying along, 'Raff's in here. However did he——?'

Mrs Faber's forefinger went over her mouth. 'Sh-sh! It was me, Mrs Delaney, but whatever you do, don't let on to Mr Delaney. Only, you see, Raff misses him so when he goes away. I don't think it's fair on the poor animal. I didn't think you'd mind, my dear. You don't, do you?'

'Of couse not,' Olivia answered. 'I love the dog. But so does my husband, Mrs Faber.'

Raff was sitting up now, yawning enormously. He jumped up to the window and looked out as if eager to be moving. 'I've put his basket in the boot,' the housekeeper said, 'and his blanket's been over him down there on the floor. There's his dish in the back and his dog biscuits and tins by the dozen of his favourite food. There's a bottle of water for the journey, in case he gets thirsty. I've thought of everything, Mrs Delaney.'

Still Olivia hesitated. She knew that if she gave in Mac-aire's wrath would descend on her own head. Then she shrugged. So what if he was angry with her? There was hardly a time when he wasn't.

'I'll take Raff, Mrs Faber. It'll be a burden off your shoulders. That's what I'll say. And anyway, I'm going away, so if my husband comes storming down to my home he won't find me there, or the dog, and he won't know where we've gone. So——' Her shoulders lifted once more. She turned to stroke the dog, who lay full-length again. 'Raff, here we go, boy!'

Strangely happier now, she waved again to Mrs Faber who stood watching the car, her hands in her apron pockets, and a sad—yet glad—expression in her eyes.

CHAPTER NINE

THE journey was behind her. For the second time in her life Olivia had travelled north to the Yorkshire moors from her home in the south. The first time she had arrived in rain and a thick, chilling mist. Now it was June. Even so, the sun was obscured by heavy clouds, but the temperature, at least, was higher.

As the car bumped along the track, Raff thrust his head and lolling tongue out of the lowered window and barked. There were scents which he recognised, and almost-forgotten tastes of the countryside, hedgerows and ditches.

Workmen were busy on the roof, repairing windows, replacing broken glass. As she got out of the car, Raff leapt to the front and pushed past her. Olivia walked forward to greet a man, older than the others, who emerged from the farmhouse.

'Name's Bishop,' the man said. 'Building contractor. Working as per instructions received from you through Pete Ivens. Nice to meet you, miss.' He turned to survey the building. 'Hope we're working to your satisfaction.'

'I'm sure you are,' Olivia said quickly. 'It's beginning to look more like home already.' She laughed and Mr Bishop laughed with her.

'East, west, home's best,' Mr Bishop quoted smilingly. 'This going to be your home? Not much furniture inside.'

'I'll buy that when everything's finished.'

'Well, that'll be a week or so yet,' said the builder. 'I take pride in doing a good job, unlike a lot of people these days. But when it's finished, you can be sure it'll be fit for a queen to live in!' They laughed again. 'Well, must be getting on. Pete Ivens' father's indoors, painting and papering.' He raised a hand and returned to his work.

There was an excited yelping from the house. Olivia found Raff barking at a pot of white paint. A tall, well-

161

built man came laboriously down a ladder. 'Must be the smell or something,' the man said. 'Whatever it is, your dog's objecting, Mrs Delaney.' He looked at his hand which was covered with paint and said, 'Too messy to shake it, but I'm Pete Ivens senior.'

'It's very good of you,' said Olivia, looking round the living-room, which was in the process of being transformed by lining paper and a coating of paint. 'It's already improved it beyond belief.'

Mr Ivens nodded. 'Can't do the rooms the builders are working on, not yet, anyway. Have to do the work as the rooms become available.' He looked at her anxiously. 'All this will cost you a good bit, you know.'

'Don't worry,' Olivia assured him. 'An aunt died and left me——'

'So my son told me. That's all right, then. Just thought I'd mention it.' A whining came from the kitchen.

'That will be Raff looking for his old basket,' Olivia said. 'I'll have to get his proper one from the car.'

'I've finished the kitchen,' Mr Ivens told her. 'Hope you like it,' he added with pride in his voice.

The kitchen was greatly improved and as Mr Ivens came to stand at Olivia's side, he said, 'I've taken the liberty in here of papering over the cracks—literally,' he added, with a laugh. 'I hope you like the paper I've used. It's tough and washable.'

The pattern was appealing, with its vegetable and fruit motifs scattered among the white and tangerine squares. 'It certainly brightens up the place,' Olivia answered. 'I definitely approve.' She turned a bright smile on Mr Ivens. 'Did you choose it?'

'Well, actually, it was my wife's suggestion.' When Olivia asked him to thank his wife, he said, 'Ted Bishop and I also took the liberty of going over the generator and getting it in good working order. We needed the electricity, you see, him especially, with his drills and so on. There are lights in every room now.'

Olivia said she did not know how to thank them for all they were doing.

Mr Ivens said, 'It's nice to know someone wants to save the place. Old Atherley let it go to rack and ruin after his wife died and his family went away. Basically it's sound. It's just that it's been neglected.'

A car drew up and Olivia, curious to know the identity of the visitor, went to the door. 'Hi,' said Pete Ivens junior. 'You arrived safely, then.' He bent down to stroke the welcoming dog, rubbing his ear. 'With canine companion.'

'Come on in,' Olivia invited. Pete greeted his father, who had climbed the ladder again. 'Have you got a message for your father, or——?'

'No, just wanted to see you. I've brought the rough draft of the story you told me last night on the phone. It can be altered if you want.'

'The kitchen's clear,' said Mr Ivens.

In the kitchen, Pete drew two or three pieces of paper from a briefcase. He spread them on the table and together they read them, Pete holding a pencil. 'I hope I've made something readable from the notes you gave me over the phone last night. If there are mistakes, it's because I was worried about the cost of your long-distance call.'

'There was no need to worry, Pete. I told you, I had a——'

'Rich aunt. Okay. I've called it what you said over the phone—A Kind of Love Story. I didn't add,' he smiled, ' "without the love", which is what you also said. And I've given it not the unhappy ending, like you said, but an open ending. After all,' another smile, 'it's not over yet, is it?'

She frowned, staring at her fingers which clicked the ballpoint pen she held. 'In just under three years it will be.'

'Hey, come on. You think I'm going to sit by and watch the marriage I helped to take place just fade out, like a scene from an old film? Now, Madam Delaney, read on.'

'Please call me Olivia,' she said absently, pulling the pages towards her.

'Delighted to oblige,' said Pete.

She read out, ' "It all began the day I was lost in the mist in the heart of the Yorkshire dales." ' She smiled at him.

'Did I say that?' He nodded. 'M'm,' she mused, 'sounds promising.' Then she read on, silently, living again the moment when she had seen the light glimmering in the distant farmhouse, hearing a dog barking and barking.

She read about the man who opened the door to her repeated knocking and how frightened of him she had been. There were the lies he had told her about his being a criminal, the threats he had made to harm her if she did not go away.

He seemed, she was quoted as saying, to need his solitude so much that he had given the impression of being willing to take desperate measures to safeguard it, even so far as to drive a fellow human being out into weather conditions in which she might not survive.

The story told of her fear of him but how, in spite of everything, some instinct had told her to trust him—and how right that instinct had proved.

'I fell in love,' she read, 'from the moment he spoke to me. I knew there was something special about him, I felt his magnetism, I saw the deep intelligence reflected by his dark eyes. From the moment we met, even though he frightened me, my heart was ensnared by the essential fineness of the man I knew in my bones existed under the rags, the beard and the ill-temper which greeted me when I begged for shelter that March evening.'

Olivia read on to the end. 'He was ill,' the report continued, 'and I nursed him back to health, staying up all night and sponging away his fever. When he asked me to marry him, I couldn't believe he loved me, too, but he must have done!

'My wedding day,' she read in the final paragraph, 'was the happiest day I had ever known. I loved him so much I did not think I could love him more, but that night I discovered how wrong I was. My love for him grew even greater. And I love him still.'

'Well?' Pete demanded.

'I like it, Pete. It isn't—well, quite as I told it to you. Somehow, it's got more—more colour, more feeling——'

'I know. More drama, more appeal. That was deliberate

on my part. The women readers will identify. They'll think it's happening to them.' He squeezed her hand which rested on the table. 'I do know what I'm doing.'

She laughed. 'I don't question that. You're a hardened journalist, tough as they come, treading in heavy boots where the proverbial angels are afraid to hover.'

He lifted his fist and made a playful lunge at her chin. 'That's enough, Mrs Macaire Connal.' She coloured a little at the name. 'I'm helping you stay that way,' Pete added. She told him how grateful she was. 'At least,' he said, 'it should stop your enemies dead in their tracks. They were blackmailing you and that's a crime, but this,' pointing to the article, 'is better than taking them to court. It's not only blunting their weapon. It's knocking it out of their grubby little hands.'

Pete's father called to ask if there was any coffee going, and Olivia, remembering her duty as hostess, answered that she would make it. While she did so, Pete played with Raff who growled playfully, hurled himself at Pete's legs and then rolled on to his back.

Olivia called Pete's father and Mr Bishop, asking about the other men working in the house. 'They've brought their own,' she was told. So the four of them sat round the kitchen table, discussing colour schemes and plumbing and tile replacement and wallpaper designs.

Mr Bishop left and Mr Ivens was about to follow when he asked his son, 'Told Mrs Delaney about this evening?'

'Not yet, but I hadn't forgotten. Olivia—you told me to call you that——' Olivia nodded, 'there's a television programme on tonight, we—that is, my parents—I——' Olivia wondered at his uncharacteristic awkwardness, 'thought you might like to see it. It's being transmitted live from a concert hall in Amsterdam. The soloist is——'

'Macaire?' she whispered.

Pete nodded. 'Like to see him?'

Tears filled her eyes. 'Oh, Pete, please . . .'

He stood. 'Come around seven-thirty. The programme starts at eight. Okay?' Olivia nodded eagerly. 'I'll knock this story into shape, then go into action. Be prepared for the shock waves to reach you in about two days' time.'

'But, Pete, no one knows where I am, except you.'

'And I won't tell. But those journalists,' he shook his head, then smiled at the joke against himself, 'they'll do anything to attain their objective, even so far as——'

'Bribing?'

'Well, not exactly, but they could telephone the local post office, for instance, or even my newspaper. I'll time things so that the story will appear in the *Moorland Evening Herald* first, then next day in the national dailies. Okay?' He lifted his hand. 'See you this evening.' On his way out, he exchanged a few words with his father and drove away.

Olivia was seated in the Ivens' living-room and it was as though Macaire was with them.

Her arm wanted to make the futile gesture of reaching out and touching him. She longed for physical contact with the man behind the glamorous, magnificent, unbelievably handsome image which was creating sounds of such beauty they held mind and body spellbound.

The Ivens family had welcomed her as if she had lived in the village all her life. She was grateful for the compliment. With them she did not feel a stranger, and she appreciated deeply their understanding of her situation. They did not watch her, but they watched with her, saying nothing, listening to Macaire's playing with the same pleasure, if not the same intensity of feeling, as herself. They listened, too, with a kind of indirect pride—they had adopted him, also, as a villager.

When it was over, the soloist bowed and smiled—once, straight at the camera—then, his hand lifted by the conductor of the orchestra, he bowed again. He returned twice more in response to the tremendous applause before the picture faded and the television set was turned off. Olivia sat, hand over her eyes, trying to control the welling misery which choked her throat. With the same understanding, Pete and his parents made no demands on her. They discussed among themselves the excellence of the concert, the appreciation of the audience and the exceptional skill of the star of the evening.

At last Olivia lifted her head and they drew her into the conversation. 'He was good, Mrs Delaney,' said Mrs Ivens, leaning back in her chair and resting her head, with its near-white hair, on a cushion. 'He really is a wonderful player.'

'Didn't he hurt his arm?' Mr Ivens asked. 'When he lived at the farm, I seem to remember the post lady saying——'

'Yes, in an accident, a car accident,' Olivia said, and hoped they would not pursue the subject.

Pete, probably sensing her reluctance to talk about Macaire's past life, suggested food and drink. Mrs Ivens went to get it, saying she didn't need help, and Olivia relaxed in the armchair, only half hearing father and son discussing other matters.

Later, Pete took her home. The house was in darkness and he went with her to open the door, waiting until she had turned on a light. 'Sure you'll be all right?' he asked.

Raff came sleepily to greet them, wagging his tail in welcome. 'With Raff to guard me, I'll be fine,' she said, bending down to ruffle his fur. 'He's really quite fierce when he's aroused. Well, he barks a lot,' she qualified with a smile, remembering her own arrival at the farm three months before.

Pete laughed and went on his way. For a long time afterwards Olivia sat in a chair, eyes closed, seeing all over again the concert she had watched on television. In her imagination she could break through the barriers imposed by reality and touch the man she loved. In her thoughts the glass melted under her fingers and she was able to stroke the face she had once idolised and now loved with every part of her.

The room they had used as a bedroom had not yet been decorated. It was as if she and Macaire had just left it after making passionate love. Even the bed had not been made. She did this, changing the sheets. After washing in the bathroom, she undressed and got into bed.

The night seemed unending. She felt lonely and lost and

even though she slept, it was not a relaxed sleep. Now and then she heard Raff moving about, as restless as she was. Apart from that, there was only the deep moorland silence. And her dreams of Macaire.

All day the farmhouse reverberated with noise. Workmen hammered and plastered, climbed ladders and mixed cement. Mr Ivens started decorating the bathroom.

It was during the afternoon that Pete Ivens walked in, calling for Olivia. She replied that she was baking in the kitchen and invited him to come through. He flung on the table a copy of the day's early edition of the *Moorland Evening Herald*.

'Open it,' he said. 'Centre page spread. Complete with wedding picture by the local photographer of radiant bride and handsome, smiling bridegroom.' He sat down. 'Which, judging by subsequent events, might well one day become a collector's item.'

Hand shaking, Olivia turned the pages, to flinch a little at the picture which seemed to jump from the page and dance in front of her eyes. Herself and Macaire, Macaire still bearded, her face smiling up at him, eyes adoring. His looking into hers, warm, aware—and just a little mocking? She had been so happy, she hadn't seen it at the time.

'Pete,' she said breathlessly, indicating the two pages, 'it seems so much, all about us, spanning such a short period of time.'

'Make no mistake,' said Pete, 'Macaire's a musician of international repute. He's been praised and admired and celebrated wherever he's gone.'

Olivia read every word of the text, then turned anxious, doubtful eyes to Pete. 'It's good, every word is true, but——'

'It'll call your enemies' bluff. That's what you wanted, isn't it?'

Olivia nodded. 'But could it—just possibly—hurt him?'

'Macaire? If it's the truth, and you assured me it was,' she nodded vigorously, 'how could it harm him?'

'Is this what's going out to the national papers?'

'It's gone this afternoon, complete with picture. To-morrow morning you'll open your daily newspaper and wham—it'll be there. Of course, what they choose to use or leave out is their concern. My guess is they won't leave out much.'

Olivia did not tell Pete she hadn't ordered a daily paper and had no intention of doing so. She did not have the courage to tell him that, now she had taken the enormous step of publicising such an intimate part of Macaire's private life she was afraid of the consequences.

Would the press seek her out, not only the national, but also the world's press? How would they discover where she was? She had not given her address to anyone, not to Mrs Faber, nor to Daniel and his mother. Only Pete and his family knew where—and who—she was. And Pete, at her request, had sworn them to secrecy.

Pete got up to go, having refused the coffee Olivia offered. 'I'm on my way to an interview. I just called in to show you the feature we wrote together.' He closed the newspaper and left it on the table. 'You know, you've earned me quite a lot of money. I feel I ought to share it with you.'

She shook her head. 'It's kind of you, Pete, but I——'

'Don't need it.' He went through the living-room, calling a greeting upstairs to his father. 'Well, the best of luck, Mrs Macaire Connal. I hope things work out for you. I hope I've helped and not hindered a reconciliation.'

'There won't be a reconciliation,' she said. 'Macaire and I have parted, officially. Eventually he'll be able to marry the woman he really wants to decorate his life, both public and private.'

'*He* wants? Are you sure you're not mistaken?' Quite sure, she told him. 'Then why did he marry you?'

'Because,' her brow pleated—it hurt to have to admit the truth—'because I——'

'Because you were there?' He threw back his head and laughed. 'Have you ever looked at yourself in the mirror?

Really looked? If you had, you'd have seen what a beautiful specimen of femininity you are. If you'll pardon the expression. Why else was that bitch Brambella so jealous of you? I speak as a hardened journalist, of course—but with a very soft centre!' He lifted his hand and sprinted to his car.

It was next morning that the world's press beat a path to the farmhouse door. As car after car drew up, Olivia, who was upstairs, having talked to Mr Ivens about colours for the bathroom, gazed out and watched them unbelievingly.

'Mr Ivens,' she rushed back to the bathroom, 'what shall I do? How did they find out?'

He came down the steps, having finished the ceiling, and wiped his hands on a paint rag. 'It was in the *Evening Herald*, remember,' he said. 'It wouldn't take much intelligence on their part to find the paper's address, ask where Atherley's Farm was and make straight for it. After all, you were missing from everywhere else.'

Dismayed, Olivia took deep breaths to steady her heartbeats. 'I've never dealt with the press, Mr Ivens. That is, apart from Pete, and he's different.'

Pete's father laughed, unfastened his paint-stained overall and removed it. 'I'd better be off. No place for me here with this mob. Who knows, they might even begin to get suspicious about me being here! After all,' he laughed, 'we're alone in the house ...' He saw to his paints and brushes.

Raff, downstairs, was barking with his usual fury. The knocking on the door had turned into hammering.

'Alf Bishop's not come yet. I'll give him a ring and warn him to keep away today. Sorry, Mrs Delaney, to leave you alone with that pack of wolf-hounds down there. If Pete hadn't gone on an interview, I'd have contacted him and got him to come and protect you.'

Raff was yelping now, he was so angry with the would-be invaders. Mr Ivens escaped unobserved through the back door and Olivia was left alone to face the press.

She had no time to comb her hair or change from the

tightly-buttoned check shirt and faded blue summer-weight pants. She looked what she was—an uncomplicated, gentle, attractive young woman who had, by accident, found herself married to one of the most celebrated concert pianists of the time.

As she eased open the entrance door, with Raff barking hysterically at her side, three faces pushed towards hers. 'Is that dog safe?' one of them asked. The door was pushed open a little more.

'Is he accustomed to strangers?' asked another, with a pronounced foreign accent.

'Will he rip me to pieces?' enquired a third, putting his foot firmly against the door.

'He'll—he'll bite you all,' said Olivia, her fear showing in her enlarged eyes. 'He hates people he doesn't know. He'll tear you to little bits, all of you. So will you all please go away?'

'Hey, dog,' said another who had pushed between the others, 'like chocolate?' Raff loved chocolate and chewed the melting square, squatting on his haunches and waiting for more.

'Traitor!' Olivia muttered, and tried to close the door against the shouts of laughter. Then the room was invaded, the door pushed shut and Olivia was in the centre of a circle. Someone discovered the only chair and with deep courtesy lifted it across to Olivia and urged her down. Raff flopped at her side. For the first time in her life she found herself the subject of a press conference.

She felt sick with fear. Pete had told her of the tactics of journalists, how they framed their questions to get the answers they wanted; how they tricked people into telling them what they needed to know; how they caught people off guard and, that way, were told what would otherwise have been carefully-guarded secrets.

'That story you told the press, Mrs Connal——'

'It wasn't a story. It was the truth.' She reached stiffly down to twirl Raff's ear.

'There's a tale going about that you're already parted from your husband. Is that the truth, too?'

'N-no comment.' Oh, no! she thought. They'll take that as an admission that it's right. 'Except that it's wrong.'

'Miss Brambella—is it true she's going to marry him after your divorce is through?'

Her head turned sharply. 'Who said anything about a divorce?'

'Your husband's alleged to be on a concert tour of Europe. May I ask why you're not with him?'

She answered sharply, 'That's my business. And his,' she added a little belatedly. A quick glance round showed her pens and pencils flying across notebooks, pocket cassette recorders switched on. She had hardly said a word, so what could they be writing?

'Annetta Brambella was there,' someone tossed at her casually. It was like a bullet passing through her heart. That moment half of her died. Somehow her composure remained stable and she answered evenly. 'She's a musician colleague of my husband's, isn't she?'

'Is she?' was the reply. 'You tell me.'

Olivia rounded on the reporter, then cursed herself for revealing her anxiety. 'I'm telling you nothing.'

The man shrugged. 'Okay, lady. Just relax.'

'This place,' another said. 'It's being redecorated, isn't it? Are you going to live here permanently?'

'Alone?' asked someone else.

'I'm not alone,' she side-stepped. 'I've got Raff.' At the mention of his name, the dog's head came up. There was general laughter.

'No one else?' another voice probed. The door burst open and Raff made a howling dive at the late arrival. The dog seemed to go mad with joy. 'Not even that boy-friend of yours,' the questioner persisted, 'to keep you warm in your husband's absence?'

Olivia snapped, 'That's an impertinent question and a violation of my privacy.'

Someone came pushing into the room, a tall man, distinguished, dark-eyed, broad-shouldered and furious. He made his way to the stupefied girl at the centre of the circle. 'What the hell,' said the newcomer, 'do you miserable lot think you're doing here?'

Lights flashed, cameras clicked. The great man himself had arrived.

'Macaire?' Olivia whispered, standing unsteadily, her face drained of colour. The shock of events was coming through, taking her completely by surprise. She started to shake and she stood helplessly looking up at her husband. His arms came round her and she found her cheek pressed against his chest. Flashlights burst whitely in the dim room. Her arms went round his solid, reassuring body and she relaxed against him, totally at peace.

'The Happy Ending,' said a brittle voice, 'with the T and the H and the E in caps.'

'Get out,' said Macaire over Olivia's shoulder. 'The lot of you, out.' It sounded to Olivia as though he was addressing his dog.

'You might regret turning us away, Mr Connal,' said one of the men.

One arm dropped from Olivia. The other held her fast, *'Regret?'* Macaire rasped. 'My only regret is that I didn't arrive sooner.'

'We were invited in,' the man persisted.

'You weren't.' Olivia's head came up. 'You pushed your way in uninvited.'

'Which means you're trespassing on my property,' Macaire retorted. 'There's the door, gentlemen of the press. Please use it.'

'We could hurt you, Mr Connal. We could blow this story up——'

'I gave you no "story",' Olivia cried. 'Whatever you printed you would be inventing.'

'Say what the blazes you like,' said Macaire. 'I'm not frightened of you. I'm fireproof. If you take away my reputation—which you can't—I don't give a damn. I've got my wife.' He lifted her chin. The cameras flashed. 'She's all I need.' He kissed her gently. Her arms crept round his neck. The cameras went mad.

When Macaire lifted his head, he seemed to have changed his tactics. 'Exercise a little discretion, gentlemen.

Use a bit of tact. I've just got home from Holland and I haven't seen my wife for some time. Get it?'

There was general laughter. The good humour of the press seemed miraculously to have been restored. One by one they filed out, one or two glancing back at the couple still locked in each other's arms.

CHAPTER TEN

WHEN the door closed and the cars had gone, Macaire's arms loosened and fell away. He turned from Olivia and went from the room, leaving her standing alone. Raff had followed his master.

Olivia put shaking hands to her cheeks, finding them burning.

Bewildered by the change in Macaire's attitude, she picked up the chair and automatically replaced it where it belonged.

There was the chink of mugs from the kitchen. She found him there, making coffee. He asked if she wanted some, but she shook her head. 'Mac?' she said softly, but he did not respond. 'Is there something wrong?'

He stirred his coffee, drank a little and stared out of the window. He had taken off his jacket and the silk shirt clung to his skin as if he had hurried and his body was still moist. His shoulder blades tautened the material. The muscles of his arms had strengthened with the exercise he must have taken in order to return to top playing form.

'Why don't you speak to me?' she said sharply to his implacable back. 'What was that loving husband act for back in there? To please your fans via the press, to allow the papers to print pictures of you as the great lover—or, more probably, to make your girl-friend jealous?'

He turned on her, swilling some drops of coffee over the rim of the cup. His eyes were ice chips, his mouth a hard line. 'You can talk about act! When I arrived, you were revelling in the attention of the world's press, playing the loving little wife role as if you were born to it. You were parrying those journalists' leading questions like a hardened celebrity, and enjoying every minute.'

He ignored her shaking head.

'You know what they'll do to you? They'll mince you into

little pieces in their machine like they do to everyone they can lay their muck-raking hands on. As they did to me when my marriage to Annetta Brambella was called off, when I had my accident and, thanks to you, they'll do it again, now—as a result of that crazy, damfool press release you handed out about our first meeting and our marriage.'

'You don't know why I gave Pete Ivens that story. Nor do you know why I let him give it to the national papers.'

'Don't I?' He threw some coffee down his throat and put the mug on the table. 'Let me make an inspired guess. You were jealous of my fame and wanted a share of it yourself, so you thought up a way of getting that share which simply couldn't fail—by revealing the secret life of Macaire Connal and the girl he was mad enough to marry.'

He looked her over, noting the casual shirt, the well-worn slacks. His eyes rose again, lingering on her hard-boned hips, the trim waist, the full curve of her breasts straining against the shirt fabric.

He moved slowly towards her, loosening his tie. With each of his footsteps her muscles tightened. He put out a hand, slipped it under her waistband and tugged her towards him. His other hand closed round her throat and his lips lowered to hers, giving her a hard, careless kiss. She jerked back her head, but he held her tightly. 'I want another,' he said.

Her arms, which had hung stiffly at her sides, came to life. They pushed at his chest, pressed into his shoulder blades, moved to his wrists and pulled at them vainly. Then she dug her fingernails into them and he released her, hurling her from him. She staggered backwards, regaining her balance only just in time. His hands, his wrists were precious to him. They were probably insured for a large amount of money.

'You bitch,' he muttered, through his teeth. 'Just like a woman—get at a man through his most vulnerable point.' He rubbed his wrists one at a time, then he snarled, 'Did it do your ego good to tell the world about your close relationship with an internationally-known musician? Did you think that by flaunting in print your so-called "love" for him, he'd forgive you for all the lies you've told him in the past? Not to mention the touching love affair on the side with that "solid, dependable" man who wouldn't "turn you away"?'

He looked around the kitchen. 'Who paid for all this re-decoration? Who paid for the repairs I could see when I came in? Who's providing the money to re-furnish the place? That *solid, dependable* boy-friend?'

'It will probably disappoint you to know,' she hit back, 'that I'm paying for it myself.'

'Another lie?'

'No,' she shrieked, maddened and crazy with unhappiness and disappointment, 'with *my own money*.'

His eyebrows lifted coolly. 'Have you sold your house?'

'No. I'm using the money my aunt left me.'

'My God, she's rolling in it! I married an heiress! Lucky me.'

'Stop being sarcastic,' she cried. 'I'm not an heiress. I never told you my aunt was poor.'

'Nor did you tell me she was rich. Another lie—by evasion.'

'You never asked about my circumstances, you were never interested enough. You didn't marry me for love—you told me that. You married me because you wanted a woman, and I was there, and because I wasn't the sort to sleep around you had to make it legal. With your ring on my finger, I came to you like a lamb. I must have been crazy, crazy ...' She slumped into a chair. Her head rested on her arms on the table and she sobbed quietly.

He made no move to go to her. It seemed he had been drained of all compassion because he went on tauntingly, 'Well, that press release might have put a pile of money into your journalist friend's pocket, but where the person it was aimed at is concerned, it misfired with deadly accuracy.'

Her head came up, revealing streaming cheeks. 'How do you know?'

'I should know my own thoughts.'

'You? You think it was aimed at you?' She shook her head. What use was it telling him Annetta had been the target? That would make him even angrier. After all, he loved the woman, didn't he? She turned her head to hide her face. She did not want him to see her apprehension. 'What do you intend to do about it?' she asked. 'Divorce me?'

'I thought that was the eventual object of our separation.'

Olivia felt herself go cold. 'But you let the press take pictures of us kissing. You gave them the impression that you wanted me to yourself. Which could be taken to mean that we haven't yet really separated.'

He shrugged. 'Do I take it that you want me to leave so that our official separation can begin all over again? Well, too bad, lady. I intend to stay the night at least.' He eyed her in minute detail. 'I want you once more. Then, when I've finished with you, you can go staggering to your "boy-friend"—and see if he can come up to *my* standards in satisfying your sexual appetites.'

He unbuttoned his shirt, walking towards the bedroom. Olivia followed. He threw his shirt on the bed and she found her eyes riveted by the breadth of his shoulders, the leanness of his waist, the magnetism of his hard, male body which drew her as if she were mesmerised.

His eyes narrowed. 'What's the matter? Can't you wait?'

If she hit him she knew what his lightning reaction would be. She could only defend herself with words. 'If you touched me now, I'd feel defiled.'

He drew in his lips. 'Why, you——'

'You took Annetta Brambella with you on your concert tour—one of those reporters told me. You think I'm so simple I couldn't guess that you took her to bed? Surely you don't really believe I can't wait for you to make love to *me* after you've slept with her?'

He was about to speak, but she went on bluntly, 'I'm willing to release you to marry the woman who slipped through your fingers nearly two years ago.'

'How kind,' he said sarcastically. 'But also how typical

of a woman to twist the truth so as to shift the blame on to the man's shoulders.'

'Blame? I'm not blaming you for anything. If you prefer her to me, I understand.' She had to pause to control her voice. 'I'm willing to go through with the divorce for your sake.'

'For *my* sake? So unselfish,' he drawled. 'So touching!' His lazy tone disappeared and he rasped, 'There wouldn't be a more honest reason—to rid yourself of a husband you took on without giving enough thought to what you were doing, and afterwards, marry mother's boy Watling?'

'No, there wouldn't!'

He went to the door, having pulled a towel from a pile in a cupboard. 'Go tell that to the dog,' he derided. 'He might believe you.' At the door he turned. 'Shall I tell you why you married me? Because deep in your subconscious mind you recognised who I was—the man on the poster on your bedroom wall, literally the man of your dreams, except that, unhappily, for you, the dream turned into a nightmare.'

It was, for Olivia, a day of mounting tension. She tried to think of a way in which she could avoid sleeping beside Macaire that night. His cold, calculated statement, 'I want you once more', rang in her head, following her everywhere, like Raff.

Macaire wandered round the farmhouse, inspecting the repairs, looking at the redecoration, examining floorboards, cupboards and even the loft for woodworm. It seemed that Mr Bishop had thought of these things, too, because much of the wood in the building had already been treated for such pests.

Macaire told Olivia of this during an otherwise silent midday meal. Over coffee she said, 'I saw you the other night on television. I thought——' she moistened her lips with a drink of coffee, 'your playing was—the best I've ever heard.'

It took him a few seconds to answer. 'Thanks,' was all he said.

'It was in Amsterdam?' He nodded. 'How did you get back so soon?'

He smiled faintly. 'It's not the other end of the world. I flew back after the performance.'

'But you told me you were going on a tour of Europe.'

He smiled again, but with a difference. 'Most of the concerts have been pre-recorded.'

'So you said it to fool me into thinking you'd be away a long time?'

'Why are you so annoyed? Has it spoiled your plans? Were you expecting mother's boy to come and keep you company? And with only one bed in the house. Tut tut.' He shook his head slowly and jeeringly.

Olivia pushed back her chair. 'Oh, go to—to blazes!'

He stood, too. 'So ladylike. Why don't you let yourself go and say the much stronger, more effective words in your not-so-pure mind?'

He strolled towards her and she lost control, hurling herself at him and hitting him wherever she could reach. He ducked so expertly and she missed so often, tears of frustration blinded her. 'I hate you, I hate you!' she screamed.

He reached for her wrists and held them together above her head. 'Yes?' he said conversationally. 'Well, since you already detest me, I might as well give you yet another reason for adding to that hate.'

He released her wrists and swept her into his arms, striding with her to the bedroom. He dropped her on to the bed, pulled at her shirt-blouse so that the buttons flew open, and dragged the garment from her writhing body. Then he gave the same treatment to the rest of her clothing.

Before she could twist off the bed and run from him, he had discarded his own clothes and was beside her, caressing her, holding her thrashing limbs still, and making her mouth his own. When he lifted his head, she cried out,

'No, no, Mac. I haven't been taking—I'm not——' A deep, sobbing breath. 'I might have a baby!'

His head came up, his eyes alight with a curious kind of

anger. 'Do you think I care?'

Her eyes held his, and in their depths she caught an elusive, tormenting glimpse of the child they might have, with his fine, sensitive features, his high-boned facial structure, his dark, unfathomable eyes, his touch of genius. A baby that would be part of him to cherish and love when he had gone from her side.

A baby, she thought, closing her eyes, a baby with such a father, a man she loved beyond even herself . . . Slowly her muscles slackened, her limbs loosened, her desire uncurled, her body yielded to his lovemaking, responding to the feel of his limbs against hers, the coaxing caress of his hands, the devouring possessiveness of his lips all over her and finally, triumphantly fastening on to her mouth.

At the height of her joy, she cried out his name. He imagined it was in protest, an expression of fear of the possible consequences. He moved away, saying disgustedly, 'Is the thought of intimacy with me so horrifying to you you have to close your eyes? Were you making it more tolerable for yourself by summoning up the features of another man?'

Bewildered, she lay still, forcing back the tears. She wanted to shout, I *want* your baby, no one else's in the whole world but yours, yours . . . That's why I closed my eyes—because the thought of having your child was so wonderful it was almost too much to bear.

He swung off the bed, dressed in old jeans and a roll-necked sweater and went from the room. Summoning her energy, Olivia dressed quickly, going into the kitchen. Macaire was reaching for Raff's leash. He wore a short jacket, zipped from the waist. His jeans were pushed into boots.

'Where are you going?' she asked tonelessly.

'Where do you think? A walk. And I don't want company.'

Frustration, misery and the anguish of yet another rejection snapped her control. 'I'm aware of that,' she shouted. 'It's a lesson you taught me just after we were married. I had to learn that you needed your solitude as much as others needed people. You were a recluse, a loner, a hermit, you said. I was told to stay out of your world. All right,' she watched powerlessly as he went to the door, Raff snapping in his excitement at the prospect of freedom, 'go for your walk. Go alone. Enjoy your solitude and,' she screamed at him as he closed the door and she wrenched it open again, 'I don't care if you never come back!'

Raff leapt and barked at her joyfully as he trotted at his master's side.

At midnight, Macaire still had not returned, and Olivia was almost ill with anxiety. Had he taken her at her word and decided not to return? Hadn't he recognised the desperation in the words, the taunt, the desire to hurt him as he was hurting her?

It was no use, she could not stay in that farmhouse, ragged with worry, while the clock moved inexorably into the small hours. It was madness, she was crazy, but she would go out and try to find him. She dressed in warm slacks and a quilted jacket over a high-necked sweater. In her car was a flashlight and she slipped the car keys into her pocket, closing the farmhouse door behind her.

With the light flashing in front of her, she walked along the track towards the road, then remembered that the track ran the other way, too, past the farmhouse and up on to the moors. She retraced her steps, having convinced herself that that would have been the way Macaire had chosen to go.

Soon the track began to climb, and it was not until she had been walking for over half an hour that she realised how futile her efforts were. In her hurry she had forgotten to put on strong shoes and the sandals she wore did nothing to protect the soles of her feet from the stones and small boulders. There were stars overhead and an almost full moon, and in its light she saw how much ground she had covered. She was in a hollow and the farmhouse had been out of sight for a long time.

She began to call, first 'Mac', then 'Raff'. Her voice echoed uselessly back. The fear crept into her mind that something had gone wrong, that Mac had hurt himself, that his arm had been injured again. This fear was so intense it drew her on and on, up and up. Her calls grew louder, her footsteps quickening. Then she found herself on a ridge. She had reached the summit of the moors which stretched dauntingly skywards behind the farm.

She lurched drunkenly on along the ridge, exhaustion dulling her reason, fatigue like a leaden weight on her limbs. Her feet came up against a piece of rock, knocking her off balance. Her sandals were too flimsy to grip and she fell forward, the flashlight slipping to the ground, her head striking one of the great boulders which were strewn abundantly across the barren moors. Involuntarily she cried out 'Mac!' and the name echoed mockingly all around her. As consciousness slipped away, she thought she heard —but knew she had imagined—an answering shout.

It could only have been a few minutes afterwards—Mac told her later it was more than twenty-five—that a series of yelping barks brought Olivia back to life.

She tried to sit up, but Raff sprawled panting beside her, preventing her from doing so. She reached up sobbingly and hugged his neck. 'Raff, oh Raff,' she said. His gold name-tag glinted in the moonlight.

Then Macaire was crouching beside her, feeling her for broken bones. 'I'm all right,' she murmured. 'It's just my head. I hit it when I fell.'

'Bad enough to knock you out,' he commented. He seems so cool, she thought. He really doesn't care . . .

He lifted her carefully and the long walk back began. 'I heard you call,' he said. 'I answered.' So it hadn't been imagination! 'It was Raff who tracked you down.' Her arms clung to his neck, her head drooped against his shoulder. 'Why in God's name did you go out?' he asked roughly.

'To find you.' There was silence for some time. Then she went on, 'You were away so long I couldn't stand it. I thought you'd been hurt.' She lifted her head and gazed at his profile, unbending and unreadable. 'Why were you out for such a long time?'

He did not answer at once. Olivia felt the downward

tread of his feet and knew they were descending. It surely could not be much farther to the farmhouse. 'I had a decision to make. It took me hours.' Her question hung unasked between them. He answered it. 'Whether or not to get up and go, to walk out of your life as suddenly and determinedly as you walked into mine.' She longed to ask him what his decision had been.

He did not speak again, except to call to Raff, until they reached the house. He opened the door and carried her over the threshold.

'A promise fulfilled,' he said, and closed the door behind them.

They lay together on the bed, Olivia on her side, Macaire on his back, hands behind his head, staring up at the moon-washed ceiling. They wore their night clothes, except that Macaire was bare to the waist.

Olivia's body was exhausted, but her mind would not let her rest. Why was Macaire just lying there? she fretted. The barriers seemed higher than ever. She would rather, she thought, surprising herself, that he made brutal, meaningless love to her than pretend she didn't exist. At least they would be in contact. Her arms would be holding him, acting as a link through which she could communicate the depth of her love. How long would this sterile separation go on? All night, until he left in the morning?

'I—I came after you, Mac. Doesn't that prove I love you?' Silence greeted the question. 'I nearly went mad with worry when you didn't come back.' She paused and her hand wandered to the bump on her head.

For a few seconds his head turned to watch her, to seek for signs of pain. There were none, and he seemed to lose interest.

'I paid for the decorations and the repairs with my own money,' she went on, 'no one else's.' She waited, then continued, 'That photograph of myself and Daniel at the concert hall in London was set up by Fulton Hallinger.' She turned her head and saw the hardness of his profile. 'Didn't you guess? You'd just sent me away. I had to have sympathy from someone. Daniel just happened to be there. That's all it was.'

He still did not respond, seeming content to let her talk as if it were the easiest way to deal with the situation.

Her voice was growing more tired. 'That day I went to Fulton's office to find out where you were, so that I could take you up on your invitation to join you——did you really know I was there?'

'Yes.'

He spoke so detachedly that anger began to override her fatigue. 'So it was true you refused to see me? Why?'

It took him a few moments to answer. 'Revenge. Because I thought your boy-friend was living with you.'

'That darkroom business? It was my aunt who first encouraged him to use it. But Daniel wouldn't have dared forsake his mother, or defy her. She's so possessive towards him, she'll never let him go. He'll grow into a crusty old bachelor.'

'Is that why you decided to marry me——as second best to the man you couldn't have? Is that why you're seeking consolation with me now?'

She raised herself on her elbow, her body tense, her lips trembling with anger. 'Why did you take Annetta to Amsterdam?'

He was unmoved by her challenge. 'Let's get it right, shall we? I didn't take her. She came.'

She flopped back helplessly. 'What's the difference? You still allowed her to go with you.'

Now he challenged her, 'Why did you tell our story to Pete Ivens?'

'You really want to know? You won't like it. It shows up your girl-friend in a bad light.'

'Carry on,' he responded evenly.

'All right. Annetta told me that if I didn't stop seeing you, she'd put her threats into practice and tell the press all those lies she'd concocted from the story she got from Mrs Faber. She would ruin your career, she said. So,' Olivia's voice rose with a remembrance of pleasure, 'I called her bluff. I told the story first——the true one.'

He stirred at last, rolling on to his side. 'Thus protecting my career?'

'And your reputation.'

'Which means so much to you?'

'Shouldn't it? I am your wife.'

'You're saying that so often, I'm beginning to believe it.'

His remark puzzled her. With dismay she watched him roll off the bed and go to the window. He stood, tall, powerful, body outlined against the moonlit panes. She wanted to run across and rest her cheek against his back, pressing herself against him and running her hands over the broad toughness of his shoulders, down to rest softly against his narrow waist.

He spoke at last. 'Annetta's taken everything from my house that belonged to her, which included a large part of the furniture and carpets.' A pause, then, 'I was glad to see them go. I never did like her taste.'

'But you were going to marry her.'

'True, but looking back, and'—with an incomprehensible glance at the still figure on the bed—'in the light of what has happened to me since, I now know it would have been a marriage without love.'

'But Mac,' she sounded as puzzled as she felt, 'you loved her, you must have done. When she went off with that other man, you had that crash.'

His voice was strained as he answered, 'That accident had little connection with Annetta, except in one respect. The night of the accident I'd given a poor performance. As I drove home, I was trying to work out why. In the end I concluded, as everyone else did, that it was my loss of the woman who was to be my wife that was the cause. It was only at the moment of impact—as a result of my straying attention—that the truth hit me. But my subsequent unconsciousness blotted it out. For a long time I was too ill even to try to recall it.'

There was a long silence and Olivia waited, her breath shallow with impatience.

He continued at last, 'When I thought my arm was so badly injured I would never play again, my resentment against Annetta began to build up. By the time they told me that there was no physical reason why one day I shouldn't play the piano as well as I'd ever done, I had lost my desire to do so.

'I found this place by accident. I bought it because it gave me the only thing I really wanted—or so I thought—solitude. It was during my months of solitary living here that I remembered what I had realised at the moment of the crash—that my relationship with Annetta and her attraction for me had been on the physical plane only and that emotionally she had left me cold.'

Olivia sat on the bed, hugging her knees. 'But the crash,' she persisted.

'I told you,' he answered irritably. 'I was immersed in my thoughts. I'd recognised the reason for the lowered standard of my performance. I'd let Annetta, with all her nonsense, plus the subsequent publicity, get under the skin of my musical concentration. It was during my convalescence that my bitterness against Annetta—against women in general—grew to such proportions that I vowed to have nothing to do with them in a personal way for the rest of my life.'

'Then,' she whispered, 'I had to come along and spoil everything for you?'

'You had to come along.'

'I'm sorry.' It was a simple yet sincere apology. He ignored it.

There was such a long silence, Olivia scrambled from the bed and tiptoed to the window. 'Mac?' She stroked his left arm. 'I'm so very glad your arm has been cured.' He said nothing. 'When you were ill with that fever and I nursed you, you called out and I'm sure it was to a woman. You said, "Don't leave me now", and "When you walked away part of me died ..." I didn't catch the name. I assumed it belonged to the woman you'd lost, but if what you say about not loving Annetta is true, it couldn't have been her, so who——?'

'You want to know?' He folded his arms and leant with his shoulder against the wall adjoining the window. 'It was you. I told you to go because I knew the moment I set eyes on you that you'd be a threat to my peace of mind. The morning you went away, I thought you'd gone out of my life for ever.'

'If only I'd known,' she murmured.

He went on, 'I knew you'd make first for the village to find someone to tow your car. I also knew you'd have to come back past the track to this house to get at your car. So I forced myself to face that mist, although I was almost too weak to walk. I took Raff and left him at the junction of the track and the road. I let him get your scent from the towel you had used, then gave him strict instructions to sit, after which I returned here and waited for you.'

She whispered incredulously, 'You knew I'd come back?'

He said simply, 'Let's say I believe there's a great deal to be said for telepathy.'

After a short silence he continued. 'In my fever I was talking to you, calling to you, persuading you to return. You, the girl I knew I wanted to have by my side for the rest of my life.'

Olivia was too choked to speak.

He half-turned towards her and his eyes softened as he gazed into her upturned face. 'Shall I tell you something? You've enriched my playing. Last night in Amsterdam, I played for you. I felt you'd be watching. At the end, I knew I'd never played better in my life.'

'Mac, oh Mac,' the tears scalded her eyes. 'I told you that I'd never leave you.'

'I didn't believe you. I wouldn't let myself, even when you told me you loved me. I asked you to marry me because I wanted to tie you to me. Then I discovered that the "boyfriend" to whom you'd referred so casually appeared to be living with you. I nearly went crazy with jealousy—and a determination to have my revenge once and for all on womankind.'

'Mac,' her hand lifted to his shoulders, 'you said to me when I came here, "Warm me, let your warmth bring me back to life". I'm saying that to you now, Mac . . .'

It was as though she had touched a button and a door

had sprung open, revealing unimagined treasures. He swung round and opened his arms. Olivia swayed into them and was scooped up and carried to the bed. He threw himself beside her, pulling her the length of him, pressing her closer until she was left in no doubt as to his overwhelming need for her.

He kissed her with a possessiveness which took her breath away. His lips, his caresses told her that every single part of her belonged to him and let her question it if she dared.

'Mac, Mac,' she whispered, burying her face in the hollow of his neck, 'I do so want your baby, no one else's in the whole world but yours . . .'

'My love, my wife, my very life,' he said thickly, 'you are the woman I love with a love that can be, will be, shouted from the housetops. You shall indeed have my baby, not just one but as many as you like. And I'll tell you something else. Never, ever, will you run from me again.'

'But Mac, whenever I did, it was for your sake, for the love of you, that I ran away. I thought it was what you wanted.'

'This is what I want,' he murmured, urging her even closer, until their limbs entangled. 'Both of us belonging to each other, as one in mind and body, until time draws its last breath.' His lips found her ear and he whispered, 'Which means for ever.'

FREE Harlequin romance catalogue

This catalogue provides you with a complete listing of all the titles currently available through

Harlequin Reader Service